Strangers. With *regrets.*

"Can we really be strangers?" Camille asked.

Jack stepped closer. "We can do anything we want." His eyes took on a slow languorous burn. "As long as you're sure that's really the game you want to play."

The rhythm of her heart changed, deepened. "Jack –"

"Because, trust me, if that was the case, if we were really strangers…we sure wouldn't be standing here right now."

All these years she'd worked to carve this man from her memory, to think of him only as a boy, a childhood crush. But here, now, with the front of her legs brushing his jeans, she realised the man was far more lethal than the boy…

"We'd be in my bed," he said, and this time he touched her, put his hand to her chin and tilted her face to his. "Naked."

Dear Reader,

Legends fascinate me. Facts are fine, but I prefer stories shrouded with mystery and drenched with possibility.

I was nine years old when I first heard about Isle Dernier (Last Island). Facts are sketchy. It's well established that the Louisiana barrier island was a popular retreat for the wealthy. Some say a grand hotel dominated the island. Others say it never existed, that it never left the drawing board…

In 1856 a hurricane ravaged the island. That's fact. That can be proven. Everything else – accounts of lovers being separated and jewels being lost, of the hotel being swallowed by the gulf and the cow that remained standing – is legend.

Today Isle Dernier is a desolate, windswept sandbar. But I've never forgotten the legends – or the possibility. So let's forget about fact and pretend the island survived, that the hotel was rebuilt. Just for a little while. Just for now.

Just for Camille and Jack…and a special mystery of their own.

Happy reading!

Jenna Mills

Sins of the Storm
JENNA MILLS

MILLS & BOON®
Pure reading pleasure™

*First published in Great Britain 2008
by Harlequin Mills & Boon Limited,
Eton House, 18-24 Paradise Road, Richmond, Surrey TW9 1SR*

ISBN: 978 0 263 85984 3

46-0808

*Harlequin Mills & Boon policy is to use papers that are
natural, renewable and recyclable products and made from
wood grown in sustainable forests. The logging and
manufacturing processes conform to the legal environmental
regulations of the country of origin.*

*Printed and bound in Spain
by Litografia Rosés S.A., Barcelona*

ABOUT THE AUTHOR

Stories set in the South come naturally to bestselling author Jenna Mills. Born and raised in Louisiana, she cut her teeth early on the myths and legends of the Old South – and couldn't get enough of old plantation ruins! She started creating stories of her own as soon as she could talk, and when she mastered pen and paper, those stories found their way into notebooks. Now she's still telling stories...still captivated by mystery – and romance.

A member of Romance Writers of America, Dallas Area Romance Authors, and North Louisiana Storytellers, Jenna has earned critical acclaim for her stories of deep emotion, steamy romance and page-turning suspense. When not writing, Jenna spends her time with her young daughter and her husband, as well as a house full of cats, dogs and plants. You can visit Jenna at her website, www.jennamills.com, or drop her a note at PO Box 768, Coppell, TX 75019, USA.

As always, so many people deserve thanks for helping me bring this story to life…

My pals Cathy and Linda, for bullet-proofing.

My agent, Roberta, for believing in Cami and Jack – and in me.

My editor, Wanda, for your wise gentle guidance – and your patience!

And of course, my husband and daughter, for…well, for everything. Because that's what you are. My everything.

Chapter 1

Sheriff Jacques Savoie liked it nice and slow.

Stepping from his squad car into the stinging rain, he didn't run for the shelter of the shadowy old house, just took a moment to savor the anticipation.

He'd returned to the sleepy town of his birth for the simplicity. He'd come back to Bayou d'Espere for the easy pace, the predictability. In the spring it stormed. The summers were hot and muggy and sometimes hosted a hurricane or two. Fall brought gray skies, geese and football. Winters were mild. Snow didn't fall and bombs didn't rip through cafés. Trucks didn't blow up, and buildings didn't fall in on you.

Each peachy sunrise didn't simply mean say your prayers and see if you can live another day.

He'd come home to savor his coffee in the morning

and play catch with his dog in the afternoon, make love with his wife in the evening.

But buried deep, the soldier he'd been for the past twelve years had festered. That's why he'd thrown his hat into the race for sheriff: to channel the restlessness that had once kept him alive, before it channeled him. The life he'd come back to was not the life he'd left behind. He'd been a kid then.

Now he was a man.

Narrowing his eyes, Jack took off through the late-spring storm, the way he'd done so many times before. Except this time he rubbed a hand against the ache in his thigh—and walked.

Once the Greek Revival plantation had been the belle of the parish. Now like so many other buildings in a post-Katrina world, Whispering Oaks stood in disrepair. Some wanted to tear her down, clear the land.

But one desecration, Jack maintained, didn't sanctify another.

His foot came down against a cypress knee and twisted, but he barely felt the pain. He passed the Condemned sign he'd driven into the ground the week before, as much a dare as a command. Keep Out, it invited. And just as he'd anticipated, someone had broken in anyway. They were inside now. They'd tripped the silent alarm.

And alone in the darkness, that someone had no idea the game was about to blow up in their face.

Nice. And. Slow.

The first break-in, back in March, had seemed benign enough. Nothing had been taken. Then came the broken window at the historical society, the stolen photographs from the visitors' center, the missing files at the library.

And the fire.

It all added up to too much suspicious activity in his parish.

At the dilapidated stairs leading to the porch, Jack resisted the urge to break into a run and kick open the door. The wood was old, rotting. A good shove and it would rip from its hinges, and he'd be free to go after the fool who'd walked into his trap. It was too pathetically easy. Plant a little information, spread a few rumors, then sit back to see who came sniffing around.

Slow and steady, he reminded himself. That's how he liked it. That's what worked.

That's what kept a man alive.

Jack followed the sweeping veranda to the right, where the window he'd left unlocked stood open, allowing the wind to push rain inside.

Quietly, he bent and stepped into the darkness of the forgotten dining room.

We shouldn't be here.

The memory jarred him. He straightened and twisted around, didn't want to see her. But through the shadows she was there, blond hair long and tangled, eyes so blue and trusting.

Since when have you been afraid of anything?

Jack's fingers tightened around the Maglite he'd carried in from the squad car. But he did not turn it on.

It could be kids upstairs with blankets and pillows and a joint. For years the old plantation had been a favorite hideaway. Legend said the house was haunted, that sometimes during the dead of night, you could hear the trill of laughter—or the wail of crying. His granny swore she'd once heard horses and gunfire. Jack didn't know how many nights he and Gabe had spent with a six-pack of beer…waiting.

But he knew exactly how many nights he'd spent with candles and a bottle of cheap wine…doing anything but waiting.

We should go.

No…not yet.

From upstairs, the thump broke the memory. Pivoting, he pulled the Glock from his holster and headed for the back staircase. It was all the talk about the book, he knew. The rumors were everywhere about the true crime writer soon to arrive in town. There was even talk about a movie. Folks were whsipering about the legend again, the murder. They all wanted to be experts, included…

Jack had other ideas.

This is wrong…I told you no…

The memory circled through the darkness, softer, like the slow slide of silk around his chest. And as his foot hit the landing, his thigh, a brutally accurate barometer, throbbed—and the scent of lavender seduced. He stood there, his jeans and button-down shirt plastered to his body, his eyes narrowed and his breath hot, and felt something inside him start to slice.

Nice. And. Slow.

He'd been old enough to know better.

She…had not.

On a violent rush, he strode toward the door he'd locked just that morning, but which now stood cracked. And this time there was nothing nice or slow about his movement—or his intent. Because all he could think was fast. And hard.

Just like so many other times since murder came to Bayou d'Espere.

At the end of the hall he stopped without pushing inside the small, nearly empty room. He forced himself to stand in the warm muggy shadows, and wait. *Breathe.*

A faint light played through the narrow opening. The size and shape of a flashlight beam, it slipped along the hardwood floor and slid over the bait he'd left against the far walls. Five crates, stacked neatly, all sealed.

His blood quickened. Teenagers wouldn't be this quiet. Teenagers wouldn't be this methodical. This careful.

Oh, God, oh, God, talk to me....

Jack shoved at the memory, shoved hard. It was the house that brought her back, the house with all its nooks and crannies and secrets, the house that made him think of his best friend's wild-child sister when he needed to think only of the perp on the other side of the door.

Slowly the light returned to the first crate, and though the scrape of a branch against the window killed the sound, he could tell the flashlight had been set down. Movement then, a distorted, elongated shadow stretching across the dusty floor.

Jack edged closer. Only a few more seconds and—

She stepped from the shadows with a grace that kicked him in the gut. Tall, willowy, dressed in black, she moved with a quiet stealth, the measured steps of the last mourner emerging from the canopy to approach the gaping hole in the ground. As if she didn't want to go. But couldn't make herself turn back.

There'd been nothing stealthy mentioned in the eyewitness accounts about the break-ins and the fire. A man, they'd said. Middle-aged, slight of shoulder. Dark hair, Grace Ann insisted, but Louise swore there were streaks of silver.

The surveillance camera outside the visitors' center confirmed her account.

But this… There'd been no mention of a woman. No mention of long legs and a narrow waist, not one word about slender shoulders and a neck that looked made for a string of pearls, wisps of blond hair slipping from beneath a baseball cap. He stood there and watched her, stood there and felt the slow burn in his chest branch out to the rest of his body.

Oblivious to his presence, she stepped toward the crate he'd set out as bait. Anyone in their right mind would realize nothing of value would be left in a deserted plantation, just waiting for vandals or vagrants. Anyone with a lick of sense would know that anything that mattered had long since been removed.

Or destroyed.

Don't…

But here she was, this woman standing where a patch-work quilt had once protected from the cold and the dust.

In front of the tallest crate she put her hands to the outside and remained that way a long moment, with her face angled away from him and her body alert. Then she let out a hard breath as she lifted the large container from the stack and lowered it to the ground.

"Looking for something?" His words were slow, deliberate, laced with the deceptive laziness that had once been called his bedroom voice.

And the woman went completely still.

"Funny thing about stormy nights," he continued in that same warm, intimate tone, as if he hadn't just stone-cold busted her. "You never know what you're going to find."

Slowly, she straightened, and he realized why her clothes clung to her body.

She was as wet as he was.

"Now be a doll and show me your hands," he said.

Again, she obeyed.

That should have pleased him. He was a man who liked others to do as he said, as he wanted.

But he found no pleasure in the way she stood so unnaturally still, with her long-sleeved shirt and dark jeans clinging to her body.

Shoving at the door, he lunged into the room and stabbed on his Maglite. "Got any friends here, *cher?*" he drawled, executing a quick sweep of the space. "Or is it just the two of us?"

Raindrops battered the French doors leading to the balcony, but no sound came from within the room—or anywhere else in the house. The woman, with her feet shoulder-width apart and her gloved hands lifted, remained motionless.

The tightening in his chest was automatic. Violent crime was rare in his parish. Drunken and disorderly conduct, sure; bar brawls and marital spats. But there hadn't been a murder in—

There hadn't been a murder in a long time.

Espere Parish was lazy, but Jack was not. And with no one to watch his back, he wasn't about to risk an unannounced accomplice barging in from behind.

Nudging his boot against the door, he closed it and flipped the lock.

She made no move to fight him, but instinct fine-tuned over the skies of Iraq would not let him relax. That kind of composure…that kind of calm in the face of fire…he knew better than to trust it.

She should be scared. For all she knew he could be anyone. He'd found her alone in the middle of nowhere, late at night with a storm raging outside. By the time he finished with her…

The thought sickened. The lightning had long since moved on, but in his mind it flashed with vicious brilliance, and for a punishing heartbeat he was in Florida again, standing in the Medical Examiner's office. Trying to breathe. Praying the body wasn't that of his best friend's sister.

Cold. That's what he remembered. The kind of bone-deep cold that spread like a toxin through every cell of the body.

The woman—the girl, he corrected—had not died a pretty death. And she had not been the woman he'd been looking for.

But this woman just stood there, *just freaking stood there,* with her back to him. He could be on her in a heartbeat and—

Either she didn't care, or wasn't the least bit concerned.

He wasn't sure which possibility disturbed him more.

"I didn't really expect anyone tonight," he said. Finally he moved, started toward her so slow and steady that the impact of his boots against the scuffed-up wood floor barely made a sound. This was when she should have flinched. This was when she should have tensed, readied her counterattack.

The fact she didn't fired his blood in ways he hadn't

experienced since his return to Bayou d'Espere two years before.

Closer, he kept his eyes on her hands, held up and out from her body. If she so much as moved—

She didn't.

He kept right on toward her. "Here I was all set to crawl into bed when the station called." Even now, after eighteen months as sheriff, the sound of the phone on a rainy night had jolted.

"That's right, sugar. The station." He'd lunged out of bed. He'd almost tripped on Beauregard. And goddamn it, when he'd reached for the phone, his hand had wanted to shake. "You see, *cher,* there's a motion sensor downstairs, and when you let yourself on in, you also sent the sheriff a nice little announcement of your arrival. So here I am."

Finally she moved. Her shoulders dropped, as if for the first time she realized how much trouble she was in.

"Now be a sweetheart," he said from a few feet behind her, "and turn around for me. Nice…and…slow."

It had been a long time since anticipation had licked quite so deep.

But for the first time since he'd announced his presence, she denied him. She didn't turn as he'd instructed, didn't offer so much as one word in protest or explanation, in defense. It was as if she were just… waiting, for the right moment.

And through the shifting shadows, Jack smiled. Maybe some men would slip into this woman's trap, but not any man who knew Saura Robichaud. His best friend's cousin had made quite a name for herself as a P.I. by allowing men to write her off as another harmless, pretty face—and body.

"You leave me no choice then," he said. "If you don't

want to turn around, I need you to go on over to that wall, put your hands against it."

He could take her; he knew that. No matter what stunt she pulled, he could have her on the ground beneath him before she put up a whisper of a fight. He could straddle her, hold her down, make it excruciatingly clear who was in charge.

"Then we'll talk," he said, his voice a hoarse rasp. "Starting with what you're doing here."

Over the remnants of the storm, he would have sworn he heard her release a breath.

"Don't make this harder than it needs to be," he advised softly, and finally she moved, stepped away from the beam of light and toward the shadowy wall, splaying her gloved hands on the cracked plaster.

He closed in on her, stopping only when the warmth of her body whispered against his. "Good girl." The need to lift his hands and—

Not a need. He didn't *need* to touch her. Those were words of lovers, not of cops and suspects. He *had* to touch her.

"It didn't have to be this way," he said violating all training and protocol. He didn't owe this woman an explanation or apology. She was the one who'd broken the law. "But you've left me no choice here." And with the words he lifted his hands toward her rib cage.

The movement was violent. So was the hard, shuttered breath that ripped from her body. But her voice was soft, quiet. "Don't."

The single word stopped him. He paused with his hands inches from her body, while everything around him surged and flashed, twisted.

Don't.

Then she spoke again, equally soft, equally quiet. Equally damning. "We all have choices, Jacques." Slowly, she turned. "Isn't that what you always said?"

She always knew she would see him again. That was just the way of it. She always knew their paths would somehow cross. No road led away forever. Eventually everything circled back to the beginning.

But she hadn't wanted it to be here, now, this way. That's why she'd come under the cover of night. She hadn't wanted him to find her in Whispering Oaks. She hadn't wanted Jacques Savoie to find her at all. She'd wanted this reunion to be by her choosing, on her terms. She'd wanted to be…ready.

But now, standing with rain-soaked clothes plastered to her body and her hands in the air, watching the slow wash of shock bleed through his eyes, she knew there was no way she could ever have been ready for this.

For him.

"Camille." Her name was rough on his voice, hoarser than his drawled commands when he'd swaggered into the musty room in full cop mode. "Jesus, God…Camille." And there in the rich brown of his eyes, it all clashed with a violence she did not remember from before—the shock and the questions and the disbelief, the horror and the possibilities. The relief.

The accusations.

And for the briefest of moments, against the play of shadows, something else, something…tender. *Agonized.*

But it was gone before she could understand, all of

it congealing into a hard glow that jammed the breath in her throat.

"What the—" he started. "Where the hell—" And then he was reaching for her, destroying the distance and the years between them, and pulling her into his arms.

She should have stepped back. She knew that. But for a moment it felt so good and right, to be there in that room, in Jack's arms. *Again.* To hear the hard rhythm of his heart and to breathe in the scent she remembered from so long ago. He'd left Bayou d'Espere for active duty, had put his life on the line and lived through the kind of atrocities most people didn't even want to read about. But, God help her, the scent of soap and sandalwood still clung to him.

Maybe that's why she stiffened. Maybe that's why she tried to pull back. But her movement only dislodged her baseball cap, and then it was Jack pulling away. Jack lifting his hands toward her face—

Jack stepping back.

That shouldn't have hurt. It was what she wanted. She hadn't come back to Bayou d'Espere for him, knew there was no way to pick up where they'd left off. She'd always been like a kid sister to him—little Cami with her pigtails and freckles—long after she'd quit seeing him as a surrogate big brother.

She'd been warned. Her cousin had told her about the explosion that had ended his Air Force career and the accident that had taken his wife. But nothing she'd heard, nothing she'd imagined, had come close to preparing her for his eyes. Once, they'd dazzled. Now they—

She made her living through carefully chosen words. But here in this old bedroom, she couldn't think of a

single word to describe what she saw in Jack's eyes.
Violence. Regret.

Isolation.

A cop's eyes, she rationalized. A veteran's eyes.
Even as the thoughts formed, she dismissed them.
She'd seen eyes such as Jack's before, many times, in
person and in pictures. They were not the eyes of a cop,
or a soldier.

"You're real," he muttered, and the edge to his voice
cut deep. "Sweet Mary, we looked for you—"

She didn't want to hear it. "Think we can put that
down now?" She detoured him with a glance to the gun
in his left hand. A Glock, she realized. Standard police
issue. "I promise I'll behave."

She'd meant the words to be light. She'd meant the
words to break the tension, toss the two of them back
onto familiar territory. To make him quit looking at her
as if he didn't know whether to pull her back into his
arms—or throw her in jail.

But as the silence breathed between them, she
realized her mistake. Time moved forward, not
backward. The familiar territory they'd enjoyed as
children no longer existed.

"I know you have questions." Everyone did. "And I'll
answer them as best as I can," she added as a shiver ran
through her. Because of the damp, she told herself. Not
because of the memories, and not because as a child,
she'd always believed this room, where several of her ancestors had been born—and died—felt cooler than the
rest of the house. "But guns—"

Jack's eyes met hers, and in them, at last, she saw him.
Saw Jacques. Saw him tearing through a briar brush and

squatting before her, saw the lightning flash as he reached for her and pulled her into his arms, held her.

She'd been twelve years old.

He'd been fifteen.

A gun, she'd cried against his wet jacket. *God, he has a gun....*

"Jack," she whispered for the first time in what seemed like a lifetime, and on his name, her voice broke.

He flipped the lock and shoved the gun into the holster around his shoulders. Then he stunned her by unfastening it and sliding it from his body, tossing it behind the crates. "No guns."

"Thank you." And finally, finally she could breathe.

He chose that moment to move toward her again. "Christ, Camille…" He lifted his hands to her face, but retreated without touching. "It's really you."

The warmth of his body invited her to step closer. Somehow, she didn't. "It's me."

"We thought—"

"I know." She'd been gone a long time. And no one knew why, whether she'd left of her own will, or been taken. Whether she'd left at all—or been killed. Whether she was hurt, whether she even cared. If she was alive.

That reality, that truth, the pain she'd caused her family, was something she'd have to live with for the rest of her life.

"Your mother—"

"I've been with her the past week," she said, bypassing questions she wasn't ready to answer. "And Saura." At the secluded home in a neighboring parish where her mother had grown up, and her cousin still lived.

"So I'm the last to know." The lines of his face, those wide flat classic Cajun cheekbones, tightened.

Camille closed her eyes, saw her brother. Gabriel had been a sophomore at Louisiana State University when she left. Now he was all grown up, a New Orleans Assistant District Attorney. He'd left for Costa Rica with his fiancée—a woman named Evangeline whom Camille's mother adored—the day before Camille arrived. "Not the last."

But that didn't seem to mollify Jack. On a rough sound from his throat, he shoved a hand through his hair, the same pecan color as before, but thicker than she remembered, longer than he'd been wearing it the last time she'd seen him—when he'd been twenty-one and cocksure and hot to show the world that while Gator Savoie was his father, Jack was not and never would be that man's son—and swore softly.

"*Mon dieu,* Cami…where the hell have you been?"

Chapter 2

It should have been an easy question. It *was* an easy question. Where had she been? Where had she been for the past fourteen years, while her family searched and worried? While her mama lit a candle in church every Sunday and cringed every time a call came in from out of state?

Where had she been when her cousin Saura suffered a breakdown?

When her brother Gabe's world fell apart?

Where had she been when Jack—

She wasn't going to answer. He could see that in the dark haze that shadowed her eyes. Blue, he knew, the kind of soft light blue some folks compared to the sky on a summer day. He couldn't see that blue now, couldn't see much in the shadowy room, just the way she stood tall and defiant despite the fact her back was to the wall.

"Answer me." The words burned, but he kept his voice nice and slow and quiet, tender even. "Please."

Backing her into a corner, making her feel trapped, would get him nowhere.

Finally she moved. She lifted a hand to slide the damp hair from her face, drawing his attention to the freckles across the bridge of her nose. "It's not that easy."

He didn't even try to stop the low rumble of laughter. "With you, nothing is."

Her smile was slow and wide and sure, and with it, the years fell away, and he could see her again, see little Cami as she'd been before. Before she'd seen her father die. Before folks started calling her Crazy Cami.

Before she'd started throwing dragons in his path to see if he could slay them. "You shouldn't be here."

She didn't flinch, just kept watching him through those secret-drenched eyes. "I'm kind of getting that feeling."

"Damn it, Camille—"

"No." She stepped toward him, closing the distance he'd put between them. "I didn't expect open arms, Jack, not after all this time. But I didn't expect this, either," she said, glancing from him to the holster he'd tossed to the ground. "A gun?" She looked back at him. "A silent alarm?"

This is Camille, he kept telling himself. Cami. But instincts wouldn't let him relax. Every time he asked a question, she countered with one of her own.

"You've been gone a long time," he said. "A lot has changed." Things she may have seen, like the bridge washed out beyond town and the massive number of trees that had perished due to saltwater incursion, the new townhome development in the shadow of the abandoned sugar factory. But there were other changes, as well.

"Did you ever stop to think maybe that's why I'm here?"

"Then you need to turn right around and leave." The words were harsh, but out of respect for what they'd once shared, who she'd once been, he kept his voice quiet. "Because no matter what you think you know," he added, and this time he broke his cardinal rule. He reached for her, and touched, connected. "You shouldn't be here." *Not now.* With the past bubbling up. The scum who called himself a writer would want to interview Camille for his exposé.

And the man she'd tried to incriminate all those years ago would do everything in his power to make sure that never happened.

"Jack…" she whispered, with a quick glance at his hands on her arms. Then she lifted her eyes. "You almost sound scared."

It was a hell of a time for her to start making sense. She'd been gone, but he had not. He'd been here when her brother had nearly been killed. He'd been here when the man responsible had strolled from the courthouse, as though he owned the goddamned world. "Marcel Lambert—"

"Finally made a mistake, yes, I know," she said, and her eyes took on a hard glow. "He went after Gabe. He confessed, told him everything."

Everything. The truth about a legend that had haunted her family for decades, an unholy alliance to locate a religious relic that had vanished during the Civil War, lies and betrayals and deceptions, the shards of glass found on the floor of her father's study—and the bullet that had ended his life.

"And then he claimed entrapment," she added with a

core of steel the eighteen-year-old had not possessed. "And now he's living like a prince while his lawyers introduce one stall tactic after another."

While the media continued to harass her brother, speculating how far he would go for revenge. That's why Gabe had taken his fiancée to Costa Rica, to get her away from the reporters who dogged them everywhere.

"But here you are," Jack muttered. "After all this time. Do you have any idea what Lambert will do when he finds out—"

"I'm not scared of him."

"He killed your father."

"And destroyed yours," she added.

But Jack ignored her comment. Because he finally realized the cat-and-mouse game they'd been playing. The timing of her return was not coincidental. "You're here for the trial."

"I'm here for me, Jack. I'm here because it's time."

They were foolish words, and they scraped. "Time for what?"

"To get my life back."

She made it sound so damned simple.

"I need to know what's going on," she said, hugging her arms around her body and drawing his attention to the knit top clinging to her chest. She was still wet, and the room was cold. "Why the gun? Why the silent alarm? It's been a long time since anyone has given a damn what happened at Whispering Oaks."

"Like I said, *cher*—a lot has changed."

"Of course it has," she conceded, watching him, almost assessing. "But that's not an answer. What's going on? Who did you expect to find here?"

If he knew the answer to that… "Go back to your mama's," he said with an insolence that brought an immediate burn to her eyes. "Let her give you some of that gumbo you always liked…give you the welcome you want."

That he couldn't.

For a long moment Camille said nothing, just watched him as if she could sear a hole right through him. Then she released a slow breath and damn near crucified him with her eyes.

"Bayou d'Espere isn't the only thing that's changed."

And then she was gone, turning and walking away, again, leaving only the sound of her footsteps against the old wood floor, and the lingering, damning scent of lavender.

She'd forgotten.

No longer concerned with concealing her presence, Camille ignored the protest of the front door and stepped into the sauna of a Louisiana almost-summer night. The rain had stopped, but the air remained damp and thick, heavy. Thunder rumbled off to the east.

And while she should have slammed the door behind her, she left it hanging open and walked into the night.

She'd forgotten. So much. The sights and smells and feel, the taste. Survival, she supposed. The edges had to dull. If you remembered how much you loved, moving on was impossible.

But it all rushed back now, much as it had the moment she'd stepped off the plane. In some ways San Francisco had reminded her of New Orleans. Both towns had a charming mix of old and new. But while rain fell in San Francisco, sometimes a lot, lightning rarely streaked across the sky and thunder almost never rattled the windows.

It was an odd thing to miss.

It was an even odder thing to forget.

But she had. She'd missed going to sleep while the world around her rocked and rolled; so she'd forced herself to forget. Now she crossed the veranda, stunned that ferns still grew in the planters she'd tended as a child, and took the steps to the clover-covered walkway. Without even looking around, she knew Jack did not follow.

He hadn't before, and he wouldn't now.

He wanted her gone. That thought should not have stung. Fourteen years was a long time; she knew that, had told herself that from the start. But as she'd turned and found him standing in the shadows, with his hair thick and wavy, the cowlick she hadn't seen in years keeping the bangs from his forehead, something inside her had shifted.

Stormy nights were not the only thing she'd forced herself to forget.

Lifting her face to the drops of water falling from the branches, Camille closed her eyes.

No, she hadn't forgotten Jack. That would have been like forgetting how to breathe. But she had forgotten what it was like to be near him, what it felt like when her eyes met his—when his hand touched her body.

She'd forgotten—because she'd had to.

But now she remembered, and now she opened her eyes and headed for her rental car. It would be impossible to forget again, but she was older now, wiser, and she would not let Jacques Savoie deny her the closure she'd come home to find.

Rounding the corner, she turned toward the tangle

of bougainvillea and wild rose that concealed her rental. As kids—

She had her hand on the front door when the shadow in the backseat shifted to reveal a man. And for a frozen moment, neither of them moved. Bushes prevented the far doors from opening—there was only one way into the sedan, and one way out.

And they both knew it.

"Back away," came a rough voice from inside the car. "Be a good girlie and nobody gets hurt."

Camille didn't move. Wasn't sure she could. Narrowing her eyes, she stared through the darkness and saw her briefcase in the man's hands. "Put it down." Her laptop was inside. "Now."

"No can do," the man said, lunging toward the back door and shoving it open.

Maybe she should have run. Maybe she should have screamed. But Camille had run before, and it had cost her.

Shoving aside the scared girl she'd once been, the woman she'd become surged after the man—and her computer.

"Freeze!"

The single word ripped through the blur of motion, but the disheveled man twisted, using momentum to send Camille staggering into the bushes. She scrambled to her feet, but before she could give chase Jack emerged from the darkness at a dead run.

"Hold it right there!" he shouted, but the gangly man vanished into the woods. Then Jack was there, tall and hard-eyed, crouching beside her. "Camille."

Upstairs, the years separating them had gaped like a horrible chasm. But now all that fell away and for a moment he was just Jack, and she was just Cami, and he was here, on his knees and reaching for her.

"Sweet God." The rasp slipped through her like a dangerous drug. "Are you all right?"

No. She wasn't all right, couldn't be all right, not when the dark light glowed in his eyes.

"He's getting away!" she forced herself to say, taking his hand from her body as she did, and refusing to feel the warmth. "He's getting away…"

Jack didn't move, wouldn't let her stand, no matter how hard she tried. He kept holding her, kept his hands on her arms—his eyes, shuttered and alarmed on hers. And for a dangerous moment it all flashed, all those years between them, the lies and the secrets and the hurts, and she was twelve years old again—and the blood was still on her clothes.

"Did he hurt you? Are you—"

"I'm fine!" Or at least she would be—as soon as he quit touching her. "But he's getting away!" With her computer. *"Go!"*

The lines of Jack's face tightened, and the disjointed moment crumbled. "Get in the car and lock the doors." Then he took off toward the woods.

Camille didn't move. There was no reason to get in the car and lock the doors. The man wouldn't be back. She'd been warned, after all. Quite explicitly. If she returned to Bayou d'Espere—

The memory sliced through the stillness, and for a moment she was in San Francisco again, sitting on her sofa, a chai latte on the small table. The letter had looked benign enough, not all that different from others she received, except there'd been no return address. The envelope had been plain and simple and white, the address typed. The stamp that of a flag.

Inside, the single sheet of paper had stopped her breath.

The unknown sender wanted to stop a whole lot more.

She made no move to return to her car, no move to step away from the rain dripping from the canopy of oak. And as a shiver whispered through her, she made no move to warm herself.

The threats were nothing new. She'd been receiving them for years. But always before she'd been able to separate herself from them.

This time that was impossible. It was *her* father who'd been killed. It was she who'd sat crouched in the corner of his office—she who'd heard everything.

Seen everything.

She alone who had the power to make sure her father's murderer no longer walked free.

Somewhere nearby, the toads made their presence known. And the crickets—the cicadas. Night sounds, so very different from the horns and sirens she'd grown accustomed to hearing from her condo by the bay.

And when the warm, salty moisture welled in her eyes, she did not blink it away.

He found her where he left her. She stood in front of an overgrown climbing rose, a big tangled mass of branches and leaves and thorns, pulled down by showy peach blooms.

The sight should have brought warmth. The sight should have made him quicken his step, reach for her and crush her in his arms. She was here. Cami was. She was alive. She was back.

But as he drank in the blond hair, the damp clothes, his chest tightened.

"Did you catch up with him?" she asked, and with the storm to the east, the sky had cleared enough to reveal the glow in her eyes. "Did you—"

"Get back what he took from you?" Jack kept his voice nice and slow, despite the hard roar inside of him. If he'd stayed upstairs thirty seconds longer— "No."

He closed in on her, kept right on walking until he was close enough to touch. "You mind telling me what the hell that was all about?"

"I found him in the backseat—"

"I got that part, *cher,* but what I want to know is why." Why she was back, after all this time—and why she was lying.

The wince was subtle, but he saw it, even as she tried to pull back. "Why did you hide your car?" That was question one, and even though he gave it voice, he already knew the answer.

She may have come home, but Gabriel's wild child sister was still hiding.

"Why did someone break in?" The sedan was a rental; there was no reason to suspect anything of value inside. Unless someone knew the car was hers—and what she was hiding.

"What were they after?" he pressed, ignoring the way she was looking up at him.

"Jack—"

He put a hand to his thigh and squeezed. "Do you have any idea what that man could have done to you?" And finally all those hard edges pushed through, and he could see her again, staggering backward. "If I'd been just a few seconds later—" He broke off and swore softly. "What were you thinking going after him?"

"Jacques." His name. That was all she said, soft and aching, a whisper, just like moments before. No attempt at explaining—or defending. She skimmed a finger along his cheekbone. "You're bleeding."

The words came at him like a bucket of unexpected water, and for a moment all the questions fell away, leaving him looking down at her, at the way she played her index finger along the dull throb of his cheekbone. "A branch," he muttered.

Her expression softened, but he wasn't sure if she smiled, or frowned. "I didn't mean to get you hurt."

No. She never meant for the consequences to happen.

But they always did.

To the east the sky flashed and he could see her clearly, the secrets in her eyes and the moisture of her skin—the way he still held her arms as if this time he didn't know how to let go—and the scrapes along her wrists, where she'd caught herself when she fell.

With detached deliberation, he released her and moved away. "I can't help you if I don't know what's going on."

This time the twist of her mouth was definitely a frown. "No," she said quietly. "You can't."

"Damn it, Camille—"

She stepped into him and pressed a finger to his mouth. "You're going to have to trust me on this, Jack. Is that so hard to do?"

Chapter 3

He hadn't answered.

Over an hour after Camille checked into the Bayou Breeze motel, she could still see the hard look in Jack's eyes as she'd waited for an answer.

In the end, the silence had told her everything.

Jack couldn't trust her—not anymore.

After a warm shower, she slipped into a large 49ers T-shirt and a pair of sweatpants, then climbed onto the bed and sat on her knees, opened her carry-on luggage.

It was all there, safe and sound inside, completely untouched by the man who'd stolen her laptop. The man may have gotten her hard drive, but she had a backup. Several of them, actually. One was in San Francisco, locked in a safe-deposit box. Some called her paranoid, but Camille knew the value of caution.

With hands that no longer shook, she reached for the

leather portfolio and pulled apart the Velcro, lifted out the notebook. Kneeling on the faded floral bedspread, she flipped open the cover and felt the rhythm of her heart deepen as she looked at what she'd written three months before.

She'd been planning, dreaming, far longer.

Sins of the Storm
by Cameron Monroe

She didn't have her computer, but she didn't need a keyboard to write. Or remember. Flipping past the notes and questions and plans, she found a blank page and started to write.

Tomorrow she would go to the bank. There was a very real chance the safe-deposit box was still there. Her mother hadn't known about it. None of them had…not until Camille had asked her mother to retrieve several books from storage.

Once her father had loved to read to her. It had been their special time. He'd stretch out his legs and put his arm around her, pull her close. *Once upon a time,* he'd always begun, even when those words were not printed on the pages.

But then, it had always been the stories not found in any book that she'd loved best, myths and legends drenched in hope and secrets and blood. Betrayal.

By the time she was twelve, she'd outgrown story time. But one night she'd walked into her room and found him sliding a book onto the shelf. He'd turned with a forced smile and muttered some kind of excuse—an excuse that had held for twenty years, until Camille had let herself go back to that night—the last night of her father's life—and remember what she'd made herself forget.

In the book tucked next to a stuffed lamb, she'd found several slips of paper. One contained a safe-deposit box number, and she'd wondered. She knew her brother had found a key taped under the kitchen table. But they'd never known what lock the key opened.

Until now.

With only the soft light of the bedside lamp, Camille poured everything out on paper, documenting her first impressions of Bayou d'Espere fourteen years after leaving.

When she glanced up again, the clock told her over an hour had passed. Dropping the pencil, she opened and closed her fingers—and saw the envelope.

Small and white, it lay on the floor just inside the door. And before she went to it, slid her hand inside her T-shirt to preserve possible fingerprints and carefully broke the seal, the sight of her name typed on the front told her the contents would be like all the others.

She opened the envelope anyway, and read the five words:

Stop while you still can.

Headlights slanted across the rain-slicked highway. For almost two hours Jack had walked the grounds of Whispering Oaks, searching and inspecting. He'd moved his car and circled back, stood in the shadows. Waiting.

For the man he'd chased into the woods to sneak back, Jack told himself. For answers.

For her.

Now he took the substandard road with the same brutal deliberation he'd once taken the skies over Iraq, navigating a sharp curve with life-and-death precision.

The simple cross on the far side of the road served a stark reminder that not everyone had the same ability. Once pristine white, now it was weathered, faded. The riot of day-lilies didn't seem to care. They kept right on blooming—

He crushed the memory and crossed a defunct draw-bridge, accelerated. As a kid—

He crushed that memory, too. Because to remember anything from his childhood was to remember her. *Camille.* And to remember was to see her as she'd been then, with freckles and pigtails and jeans rolled up to her ankles, following him and Gabe around the swamp.

Those memories, of the girl she'd been, were not how he needed to think of Camille. He needed to remember her the way she'd been tonight, the woman who'd slipped back into the town under the cover of darkness, who'd chosen to visit Whispering Oaks at night, who'd gone to great effort to conceal her car.

It didn't take great deductive reasoning to realize she'd not wanted to be found—especially by him.

Jack took another wicked curve, but the images, the questions, persisted with every mile he destroyed. She shouldn't have been at Whispering Oaks. She shouldn't have been the one to take the bait. He'd floated the rumors himself, about the boxes in a locked room at the plantation—but he'd never specified what they might contain.

He'd been much more interested in who would come looking.

But he'd never expected *her.*

Now, Christ…now.

She wanted him to trust her. She'd stood there as if not a freaking day had passed and asked him to trust her, despite the fact she'd refused to tell him one word about what she was doing there in the middle of the night. Or where she'd been.

Once that wouldn't have mattered. But she'd been a kid then, and he'd loved her like the little sister he never had.

The woman he'd found tonight—tall, dressed in black with rain-slicked hair and secret-clouded eyes—was a stranger.

For fourteen years they'd looked for her, and for fourteen years Marcel Lambert had gloated. She'd been the only link between him and a murder the coroner had labeled suicide, and with her out of the way, Lambert had basked in the small fortune he'd amassed as a renowned restaurateur.

Poor little Camille, he'd pretended to lament. *Think her recklessness finally caught up with her?*

Jack clenched his hands on the steering wheel.

Any word on poor Cami? I heard they found a body in the Everglades.

On a hard turn right, he accelerated toward his house, but Lambert's words stayed with him.

You'd think if that girl was alive, she'd have come home by now….

But that had been before a prostitute had been murdered and before Lambert emerged as the prime suspect. Before he'd been so certain that his plan to destroy Camille's brother would succeed that he'd confessed everything.

Before the judge had granted bail anyway.

That Camille would resurface now, with Marcel
Lambert, the man she maintained murdered her father,
facing trial—no way was that a coincidence.

Frowning, Jack turned into his driveway just as his cell
phone started to ring.

Dark blanketed the small central business district.
After midnight, no pedestrians walked the sidewalks.
The streets were still, quiet. Even the diner sat empty, its
doors having closed over an hour before.

Jack scanned the turn-of-the-century storefronts,
looking for any sign of activity, a shadow, motion…
anything.

Farther down, the blur of red and blue flashed like a
tacky neon sign. The traffic light turned red, but Jack kept
right on going, completing the twenty-minute drive to the
savings and loan in just over ten.

The crowd didn't surprise him. Word traveled fast
in a small town—and late-night calls had become far
too common.

Hank DuPree, a twenty-four year veteran of the
sheriff's office, greeted Jack as he walked inside. A tall
man with the haunted eyes of a Vietnam vet, Hank
breathed and bled law enforcement. But he'd never
wanted to be the one in charge.

Beyond him, the door to the vault hung open. The
bank manager stood in a wrinkled suit, watching deputies
sift through the mess on the floor. And the bad feeling
Jack had been fighting from the moment he'd found
Camille standing in the shadows wound deeper. "What
do we have?"

"In and out in less than five. Looks like the perp knew exactly what he was after."

The M.O. matched the break-ins at the library and the historical society; late night, targeted. "What this time?"

With an odd little smile, Hank lifted his hands, revealing a stack of old documents and photographs. "Now that's where it gets interesting, Sheriff…"

The marshmallows are melting.

Resisting the urge to take a sip of the hot cocoa, Troy Fontenot's daughter hurries down the hall. Earlier, when she'd found her father in her room, returning a book to the shelf, he'd been upset. That's why she made the hot cocoa. It's his favorite. It'll help him be happy again.

"You son of a bitch!"

Two decades later, Camille could still hear the snarled words, could still feel the way her heart had pounded. Kneeling on the bed, she clenched the pencil and kept writing, let the words flow….

She stops a few feet from the door and listens. She'd thought he was alone.

"Easy there—you're overreacting."

"The hell I am."

It's nighttime. Outside the rain comes down hard. It's a summer storm, with wind and lightning and thunder. Once she'd loved storms—but that had been before her great-grandmother's house burned. Now she just wants it to stop—

"What the hell—"

Her heart slams hard against her chest. Alarmed, confused, because her father never raises his voice, she steps toward the cracked door and pushes inside.

The gunshot stops her cold—and the mug of cocoa shatters.

Camille came awake hard, her body drenched with memory and perspiration. Sucking in a sharp breath, she rolled toward the clock and realized she'd fallen asleep. The notebook still lay beside her, the pencil in her hand. But the first strains of sunlight slipped through the curtains.

"Camille, answer me, damn it!"

She swung toward the door, realized what had awoken her. Not a gunshot. The slam of a fist.

Jack's fist.

At six-twelve in the morning.

"Damn it, *'tite chat*." He growled the words with another urgent knock. "Open the door!"

'Tite chat. The nickname he'd given her as a child— Cajun for little cat—did cruel, cruel things to her heart.

Forcing the calm she'd never mastered during those dark, broken years after her father's death, she slipped from bed and walked to the door, laid her hand against it as she pushed up to the peephole—and saw him. Saw Jack. His eyes were narrow, focused, the lines of his face tight. He'd yet to shave. He'd yet to—

"*Fils de putain,*" he muttered, pivoting toward the front office.

She fumbled with the dead bolt and the chain, yanked open the door. "Jack—"

He stopped and turned, pivoted so violently she took an instinctive step back. "Camille."

Her heart kicked hard as she saw the gun in his hand. "What's going on?"

With a quick survey of the truck and SUV-cluttered parking lot, he closed in on her. For the first time she noticed the uneven hitch to his gait. And something inside her stilled. He fought it, hid it, but it was there, the faintest trace of a limp.

From Jack.

She'd heard about the bomb, but she hadn't realized...

He took her hand and led her back into her hotel room, shut the door and turned the bolt.

And deep inside, fascination tangled with dread.

He shoved the gun into his waistband and squeezed his thigh, gave her no time to prepare. She'd imagined this so many times, imagined what the years had done to him, what *Iraq* had done...what it would be like to see him, to touch him.

But nothing prepared her for the reality of facing a man who bore virtually no resemblance to the boy she'd once vowed to love forever. His jeans may have been faded and his black button-down wrinkled, his jaw unshaven, but that's where the deception ended. There was a hardness to him now, a veil of isolation that hovered like mist on a cold damp day.

"There was a break-in at the savings and loan," he said, and though his voice was calm, quiet, she knew. Without any further explanation, she knew why he'd come to her, what he thought.

She also knew he was right.

"Live Oak?" She tried to sound only mildly curious, but inside, frustration scraped. She should have password protected the file, damn it. It had been the last one she'd accessed. All someone needed to do was open her word processing program.

It was all there, her notes and theories, questions. Plans.

"Just after midnight," Jack confirmed.

Somehow she kept her expression blank. Somehow she kept the hot frustration from consuming her. He was a cop, she reminded herself. He was just doing his job, knitting the pieces together in search of a coherent picture. "Did he take anything?"

Jack's eyes narrowed. "What makes you think it was a *he?*"

Because it had been a man who stole her computer. "Just a guess." Turning toward the automatic coffeemaker, she reached for the small pot. "From what I've read, most bank robbers are."

"I never said the bank was robbed."

She stilled, forced herself to turn toward him. He stood less than two feet away, with that unsettling stillness all cops had, watching her through eyes darker than she remembered. Harder. And any illusions she'd harbored about him not knowing—or at least suspecting her involvement—crumbled.

"You asked me to trust you," he said. "But I can't do that, *cher*...not until you start trusting me."

The slow bleed stunned her. It wound through her chest and tightened, made it impossible to breathe. "I don't know what you're—"

"Yes, you do." He eliminated the distance between them in two quick steps and reached for her, put his hands on her arms and pulled her toward him, not roughly the way a cop might manhandle a suspect, but with an intimacy that heated her blood. "Goddamn it, if you're in trouble again, you need to tell me. If someone is trying to hurt you—"

"No." She ripped away and stepped back, tried to breathe. "No one is trying to hurt me." Just stop her.

"Then how do you explain this?" he asked, and before he even pulled the envelope from his back pocket, everything inside her stilled. Because she knew. He'd found something. There in the bank she'd planned to visit in a few hours, Jack had found what Camille had come looking for.

And now her plan to slip in and out of town without him discovering her true intent was about to blow up in her face.

For a long moment, he watched her in that mistrusting, assessing way all cops had. Then he opened the envelope and dumped its contents onto the small desk. Old documents came first, the parchment paper faded and yellowed, thin, but the official seals still visible. Certificate of marriage, one read. The second: Certificate of live birth.

Hers.

"My God." Trying to process it all, to understand, she extended her hand just as the old Polaroid slipped from the envelope—and the light pink walls started to close in on her.

There'd been no proof, after all. Until now, there'd been no proof the safe-deposit box remained at the bank after so many years of abandonment. Only a hunch—and a hope.

"I remember that day," Jack said as she fingered the picture on top, of her in a pale yellow Easter dress, sitting on her tricycle with ringlets falling against her face, a stuffed lamb tucked under her arm and chocolate smeared on her cheeks. "You were three."

It took sheer determination, but somehow she breathed. And somehow she allowed herself to sift past the Easter picture to those below it, all pictures of her and Gabe, their childhood. Special pictures, taken on special days.

Special pictures that stopped because the special days stopped, nine years after the first picture had been taken.

Looking up, she found Jack watching her. "I don't understand…"

It stunned her how badly she wanted to see one flicker, one trace, of what they'd once meant to each other.

"Oh, but I think you do," he said in that horribly quiet voice. "That's the funny thing about coincidence, *'tite chat*. It doesn't exist."

Refusing to let him back her into a corner, she lifted her chin and smiled. "I never said that it did."

"You've been gone fourteen years, Cami. *Fourteen years*. That's a long time. Then suddenly you show up sneaking around Whispering Oaks like—"

"I wasn't *sneaking*."

"The bank is broken into," he continued in full-interrogation mode, "a safe-deposit box destroyed, and inside I find pictures—of you."

Put together that way, it sounded pretty incriminating.

"What was supposed to be in the box, Cami?"

The question, so abrupt and simple, the kind any cop would ask, scraped. She looked down at the table, stared at the completely benign image of her on the tricycle. "Not pictures."

One step and he was there, tucking a finger to her chin and tilting her face to his. "Tell me."

She had to. She knew that. She could lie, but he would

know. And if he so much as even suspected she was hiding something, he would keep digging until he found out. If she was the one who measured out the information, then at least she maintained some morsel of control.

"I don't know." That *was* the truth. "I…" She swallowed as the cold, slow burn of disappointment spread from her throat to her chest. "Not pictures of me."

Jack kept watching. "But you expected to find something. That's why you're here."

The sunlight slipped through the curtains, brighter now, harsher, illuminating nuances she didn't want to see. "Yes," she admitted. "I—It was my father's box. I only found out about it recently. I thought if it was important enough that he kept it a secret, then there must be something in there—"

"About the night he was killed."

"Yes." There was no point pretending.

"Last night that man took something from your car." It wasn't a question, just a statement of fact—a fact she'd deliberately withheld. "And that something led him to the bank."

And now she might never know what her father had gone to great lengths to protect. "My laptop."

Jack swore softly. "Damn it, Cami, why didn't you tell me this last night? We could have been waiting…we could have caught the son of a bitch before he got his hands on what was inside."

She turned before he could see the quick twist of frustration. "I didn't know," she said, reaching for the coffeepot and carrying it to the bathroom sink. If she'd had any idea the man who'd stolen her laptop was going to go after the safe-deposit box, she would have taken precautions. But she'd thought he'd only meant to stop her. Scare her. "If I could change—"

"Son of a bitch."

It was his voice, low, hoarse, more than the actual words, that stopped her. Slowly, she looked into the mirror and saw him, saw Jack, standing next to the night-stand between the two beds. He looked taller than he had moments before, his broad frame dominating the small, warm room. But it was his eyes that got her. They were flat and coldly furious—and before she even looked at his hands, she knew what she would see.

Chapter 4

Words. That's all they were. Black, crudely printed, carefully chosen. Insidiously clear.

Stop while you still can

Slowly Jack looked up to find Camille watching him in the bathroom mirror. She stood there in an oversize T-shirt, her hair falling against her face, looking so much like the girl she'd been.

But it was a stranger's eyes that met his, dark and secretive. *Aware.*

He moved toward her, kept his eyes on the mirror. On her. She should have been afraid. She should have been terrified. Someone had threatened her. Someone wanted her gone.

Questions twisted through him, but he kept his steps steady, measured. He didn't want to—

Didn't want to frighten her.

The absurdity of the thought burned.

Nothing frightened Camille Rose Fontenot—even when it should. Once her fondness for doing the unexpected had been cute, innocent, nothing more harmful than curtains in an all boys' fort.

Then the innocence had died, and her stunts had spun out of control.

"You weren't going to tell me about this, were you?" Over the skies of Iraq, he'd learned to shut out emotion. To focus or die. He used that now, used it to strip all those hot boiling edges from his voice.

She closed her eyes, opened them a heartbeat later. "Jack, I need you to trust me—"

"How?" The question tore out of him. "Tell me how I'm supposed to do that, when it's been nothing but secrets and lies from the moment I found you sneaking around Whispering Oaks."

"You *know* me," she whispered.

He did. That was the problem. He knew her. He knew her penchant for keeping secrets—and rocking the boat. He knew the desperation, the completely fearless determination that drove her.

"Jack," she said into the deliberate silence. "This is me, Camille. I'm the same person—"

"Trust me, I know who you are." With cold efficiency he reached around her to turn off the water. "That's why we're standing here right now." Why she wasn't downtown, in jail. "That's why you didn't bother to call me, why you sneaked back into town without so much as one single damn thought about what you might be walking into."

Turning, she looked at him with wounded eyes.

"That's why you're so scared," he added silkily. Not because of the man who'd broken into her rental, not because of the threatening note.

Because of him. Because he knew her.

He always had.

"Saura was right," she whispered, wedged between his body and the tacky little vanity. "You've changed."

He stood without moving, even as the disappointment in her voice sliced—and the smell of lavender taunted. "Time's supposed to move forward, *cher*...not backward."

The glow in her eyes dimmed. "Unless it's just one big nasty circle."

His smile was slow, easy. "Then let's try this again." He returned to the bed, picked up the note. "I'm listening."

Blond hair fell against her face. "Of course." With a briskness that surprised him, she reached for the small pot and poured out the excess water, carried it back to the coffeemaker. "What do you want to know, *Sheriff?*"

Sarcasm wasn't supposed to slip like a caress. "Everything." Where she'd been. Why she'd come home...why she'd inserted herself in Lambert's crosshairs.

"Which came first?" He looked back at the crude handwriting. "The note or your car being broken into?"

She tore open a little foil packet—dark roast. "The break-in."

Which meant there'd been time for someone to access her files, see something they didn't like. "Where did the note come from?"

With a laissez-faire that burned, she poured the

grinds into the filter. "Slipped under my door sometime after midnight."

When she'd been alone. Probably in bed. "And you didn't call me?"

Now she turned, rested her hip against the chair. "Would that have made you happy, Jack? If I'd called you?"

His chest tightened, but before he could continue the interrogation, his cell phone rang. He grabbed his phone and glanced at caller ID, jabbed the talk button. "Savoie."

"Sheriff." The voice belonged to the youngest deputy on his force, Russ Melancon…and it was shaken. "There's been an accident."

Two sets of skid marks veered off the narrow, canal-lined highway. One went right. The other went left.

Both ended in murky water.

Lights flashed and sirens screamed. Cars were everywhere. Some people ran; others stood and gaped. Margot Landry held her two grandchildren—and cried.

Jack closed in on the scene, refused to let himself run. To limp. The leg itself had healed, but the doctors had warned the nerve damage was likely permanent. With effort he kept his stride brisk, his expression unreadable, his voice authoritative. Everything was under control. Janelle and her kids had been pulled from their minivan. The little girl was crying, but their grandmother was with them. The paramedics were with Janelle. She was hurt—hurt bad. But she was alive.

So was the driver of the little muscle car who'd gunned his engine after a deputy had turned on his siren and signaled for the driver to pull over….

"Name's Hebert," Russ said. "Billy. License lists an address in Bunkie."

Jack glanced at the stretcher alongside the shoulder, where two paramedics tended the motionless man. Mid-thirties, Jack would guess. Thin. Track marks on his arms. "Find anything else?"

"Not yet. Just his wallet and the envelope."

Against the folder found on the front seat, Jack's fingers tightened. Hank had spotted the black sports car just outside town and had immediately linked it to the description of a car seen in the vicinity of the savings and loan break-in. He'd turned on his lights and signaled for the driver to pull over, but the bastard had floored the engine instead. Like a coward, he'd tried to run, to get away, tearing down the highway at a ridiculous rate of speed. He'd seen the minivan too late.

Grimly, Jack glanced toward the growing crowd on the other side of the highway—and saw her.

And the edges of his vision blurred.

Dressed now in low-riding jeans and a soft peach poet's shirt, she stood with Margot Landry. He couldn't see her face, just the way she lifted a hand to stroke the little girl's hair from her tear-streaked face.

And the slow boil worked from his gut to his chest.

"Sheriff, you want me to—"

"Go on home," he said as he twisted toward Hank, the deputy who'd initially given chase. "You took a nasty blow. You should get some rest."

Hank shook his head, even as he lifted his fingers to the gash at his cheek. He'd barely brought his car to a stop before ending up in one of the canals. "Looks worse than it is. I can—"

"Everything's under control. We can take it from here."

Hank's mouth tightened into a flat line, but he did as told—and Jack started across the highway.

She didn't see him at first. She'd gone down on a knee, was holding little Annie's hands. But he could see her, could see the concern in her eyes, the gentleness in her touch. And all those hard edges inside him started to scrape.

Abruptly she looked up, stilled as he eliminated the last of the distance between them. But it was not to her that he spoke. "Mrs. Landry," he said, and his former fifth grade teacher turned toward him with dark, frightened eyes.

"Jacq—I mean, Sheriff," she said in a voice thicker than usual. "Have you heard anything else?"

He took her hands and squeezed. *"Mais non."* Just that Margot's daughter had lost consciousness and was bleeding inside. Just like—

He shoved the thought aside, refused to go back to that cold foggy night. Instead he focused on the little boy, no more than seven years old. He stood next to his grandmother like a little man ready to take on the world.

"The folks at the hospital are waiting for her," he said. "You need any help with the kids?"

"Thank you, *mais non.* Their daddy's on his way."

Greg. He ran the local insurance agency and doted on his family. "Let me know then," Jack said, and forced himself to look down, to see Camille pressing a soft kiss to a scrape along Annie's forehead. And all those sharp edges cut even deeper. He didn't let himself touch her. Didn't trust himself to. Because if he took Camille's hand—

She didn't belong here. The thought sliced through him as her eyes darkened. She didn't belong here with Mrs. Landry, didn't belong with little Annie, shouldn't be the one comforting them, not when she could have prevented all of this with a few simple words.

"Jack—" she started to say.

He didn't let her finish. "If you'll excuse us," he said to Mrs. Landry, but before she could respond, he was reaching for Camille. She stood and stepped back, lifted her eyes to his as he put a hand to the small of her back and steered her away from the accident, toward a yellow road sign warning of a dangerous curve. Just beyond sat his squad car.

The second they were out of hearing distance he released her and stepped back. "I told you to wait for me."

"I was worried—"

"Why?" The question, in the same silky tone he used during all interrogations—*and seductions*—hovered there between them. "Because of the accident? Or what I might find?"

She stilled, even as the wind kept whipping hair into her face. "What you might find?"

"Tell me," he pressed. "Tell me what else is on your computer."

Before she could answer, a car zipped around the curve, stopped just as fast. "My computer? I don't understand—"

Greg Martine pushed open the door and bolted from the car.

"None of this had to happen," Jack said with a stillness at odds with the way Greg ran. "None of it. The break-in, the theft, the—" He broke off and glanced up the road, watched Greg reach for his wife's hand. "If you'd just told me the goddamned truth."

"Jack...I had no idea—"

He spun toward her and allowed himself to back her against the front of the car. To feel her thighs pressing against his. "But you should have." Fourteen years had gone by, but Camille Fontenot still didn't give a damn about consequences. "What else?" he asked as one of the ambulances took off. "What other little surprises are on your computer?"

Her eyes darkened, but she didn't answer. At least not with words. She lifted a hand to her mouth as Greg ran with Annie to his car. Little Greg raced behind him. "My God," she whispered. "I never..." She squeezed her eyes shut, opened them a moment later. "What about the driver?" she asked, as he'd known she would. "Was he the one?"

"Yes."

"Did he still have—" The words died off, but the question hung there in the void of sirens that had finally gone quiet. The blue of her eyes glowed with it. Her body practically vibrated. And Jack wanted to know why. Camille claimed she had no idea what her father had hidden in the box, but exposed by the relentless wash of sunshine, she reminded him a little too damn much of her own father—and of Jack's. It was the fervor...the obsession.

"This?" he asked, holding up the folder. Slowly, deliberately—the only way he allowed himself to do anything—he withdrew the plastic bag he'd tucked inside. Her eyes flared as she saw the yellowed paper. Then came the slow, brutal wash of recognition he'd known would come, the same wash he'd seen the morning he'd walked away.

"My God..." she whispered as he set the plastic bag on the car behind her. She turned toward it and braced her hands against the hood. *"Daddy..."*

Jack stepped closer, looked over her shoulder at the map her father had constructed—and his had coveted.

"All these years." Her voice was soft, faraway, and it damn near sent him to his knees. "I thought Lambert had this."

They all had. It had been the only explanation that made sense. "Wouldn't have done him any good." Camille's father had already found the stained glass.

Found. And destroyed.

But standing on the edge of the accident scene, in the sudden deafening silence, she didn't seem to hear. She dragged her finger along a straight line, much as she'd once—

He stiffened, crushed the memory before it could form.

"I used to find him in his office at night," she said, "sitting at his desk with a glass of scotch, just staring...."

Obsession. Jack knew the disease well. As kids, the legend had fascinated them: a stained glass depiction of the rapture salvaged from a church in France and smuggled to Louisiana before the revolution.

"Sometimes your dad was there, too."

They stood on the side of the road, surrounded only by water and cypress and pine. But the walls pushed in anyway. And the sun burned through the haze.

"They were fools," he said, looking beyond her, to the muscle car partially submerged in the canal. "Both of them." All of them. So driven by their quest to validate a legend that they'd sacrificed their families, and their lives.

"I remember the first time he told me the story," Camille said, but Jack didn't look at her, just kept watching Russ talk with the tow truck operator.

"I sneaked into his office and found a file open on his desk…I remember being surprised to find drawings inside."

From his front pocket, Jack grabbed his sunglasses and slid them over his eyes.

"When he found me I was coloring away."

The image formed before he could stop it, of Camille destroying without even trying. He turned back to her, found her looking south, where a few miles down the road her childhood home remained. Abandoned now, in disrepair after the hurricane…but still standing. There was an odd glow to her eyes, as if she could see through the trees and the moss, through the years….

"That night when he tucked me in, he asked if I wanted to hear a true story."

Jack remembered. He'd been there.

"I remember it all," she added so damn quietly he barely heard over the low rumble of the tow truck's engine. "The mysteries and the miracles…"

Jack had heard, too. His father had been Troy Fontenot's partner. Every night after dinner, Gator Savoie had reached for a beer. And like clockwork, after three beers, the stories had started: the stained glass window was not of this world; it could heal and it could weep, and sometimes it would bleed. Twice a year, his father had said, on the winter and summer solstice, when the sun hit the window just so…that's when the miracles happened.

You get touched by that light, boy, it's like being touched by an angel…

"Obsession," he corrected. This was exactly why he didn't want her snooping around, trying to reenact her father's final days. Marcel Lambert faced charges, but he was out on bail. And his reach was far. The second he learned she was back, that she was stirring up waters best left still—

On a hard breath, Jack pivoted toward her and reached for the map.

But Camille was faster.

The violence in his eyes, his voice, stunned her.

She held her hand over his, not about to let him yank the map away from her. Not about to let him yank anything away.

All the while she slid her free hand into her purse, where she deposited the small microcamera she'd withdrawn while Jack had been watching the Camaro being pulled from the canal. Over the years, she'd learned to be very careful.

She'd also learned to take nothing for granted.

Stay here. That's what he'd told her before he'd torn out of her hotel room. But she'd seen his eyes go flat, his mouth tighten, and instinctively she'd known he hadn't told her everything.

The second Mrs. Landry had said the words *high-speed chase,* the awful coldness had seeped deeper. Because Camille had known....

Now she looked at the hard-eyed man crowding her against the squad car and tried to see the boy he'd been, the one who'd once scoured the swamp in search of the relic he now condemned.

But the knight in shining armor from her childhood,

the one she'd loved with every corner of her young heart, no longer existed.

The reality of that cut more than it should have. This was what she'd wanted, she reminded herself, to research her book and testify against Lambert, to make sure the man paid for his crimes, then walk away. And never look back. To sever all those ridiculous, tattered ties that still bound her to this place. This man.

This stranger.

But here in the muggy, midmorning sunshine with her fine-boned and pale hand resting atop his much larger one, something inside her shifted.

"It's my family," she reminded. And the religious artifact her ancestors had smuggled from France—*that her father had given his life for*—was more than just a legend. "*My* legacy."

"And it's gone."

Her heart kicked. It had been April. She'd still been in bed when one of the national news shows had pre-viewed a segment about mysteries and secrets and greed, murder and scandal—and étouffée. She'd sat up slowly, fisted the sheets as one commercial after another dragged across the television screen. Then the anchor returned, and within ten seconds she'd been staring at her brother's face.

The shock had stolen her breath. She'd untangled herself and moved toward the set, lifted a hand and touched him. Touched Gabriel. All the while the anchor had tossed out the details of the story like tawdry gossip: a twenty-year-old family feud had boiled over down in the Big Easy, leaving a celebrated restaurateur facing two sets of charges—the murder of a young French

Quarter waitress, and the attempted murder of two assistant district attorneys. At the heart of the scandal, a storied religious artifact dating back to the sixteenth century....

"They destroyed it," Jack said now. "It's over."

Maybe for him. Maybe for everyone else. But not for Camille. And it wouldn't be, it couldn't be, until the truth about that night, until the truth everyone claimed was nothing but a figment of Camille's broken imagination, was exposed.

Lambert had confessed. He'd actually admitted everything to Gabe. When he'd thought Gabe would not live to repeat it. He claimed her father found the stained glass and attempted to double-cross Marcel and his brother, his financiers. There'd been a struggle. And the priceless artifact had shattered.

Coercion, Lambert's lawyer claimed. The man had said what he'd had to say to save his life. *From Gabe.*

The absurdity of that, the fact the judge had actually bought the claim, fired through her.

"Then what's the harm?" she asked, sliding her hand from Jack's to the faded map her father had concealed from the world. Maybe it was the one he'd used to find the stained glass. Maybe it was a decoy. Maybe it was nothing, a wild-goose chase—or dead end.

Or maybe it was something he'd died to protect. "This isn't yours to destroy, Jack. It's mine. My family's."

His smile was slow, insolent. "Sorry, *cher.* What it is is evidence."

Ignoring his smugness, she ran her finger along a line that seemed to indicate a break between land and water. The map was a close-up. All she had to do was figure out

the broader location—an area bordered by a beach?—
and she could see for herself.

"Then you better take good care of it, Sheriff," she said
with her best Southern belle smile. "It sure would be a
shame if anything happened to it on your watch."

The taunt registered in the dark glitter of his eyes.
"Trust me, *cher.*" Not Cami. Not *'tite chat.* "Nothing's
going to happen on my watch."

He watched her. She could feel him even though the
deputy did his best to be inconspicuous. He was just a
kid who wore jeans and a T-shirt and pretended to work
under the hood of a rusted pickup. But she'd seen him at
the accident scene. He'd been with Jack. He'd had a gun.

Now with a wrench in his hand, he tapped his foot to
the beat of a jangly zydeco tune.

Camille could only imagine what it was Jack expected
her to do. She glanced at the file on the hotel bed, then
again toward the window, and finally she saw the car.
Sleek and black, the convertible glided into the parking
lot and straight into a spot outside her door. Quickly she
grabbed her notebook and her purse, then slipped into the
warm blast of late afternoon.

It was like stepping into a sauna.

The deputy looked up, and though Camille knew
better, knew it was best to ignore him, pretend she had
no idea he was there, she tossed him a wink.

His flush almost made her laugh.

At the car, one darkly tinted window slowly
lowered. "Ready?"

"As rain," Camille said, opening the passenger door
and slipping inside.

Her cousin's smile, wide, conspiratorial, almost blinded her. "Thought I'd wait to lower the top until we were out of here."

"He'll get the plates," Camille pointed out.

Saura laughed. "But until then he'll sweat a little." She zipped the car backward, then slid into Drive and sped forward, gunning the engine as they turned onto the highway.

And for the first time since she'd returned to Bayou d'Espere, Camille could breathe. She rolled down the window and welcomed the slap of warm air as the outskirts of town raced by in a blur.

"That bad?" Saura asked.

Camille lifted her hand to the open window. "He knows," she said. "He knows there's something I haven't told him."

"Then maybe you should."

"Not yet." Not until the last possible moment. Doors would open for Camille Fontenot…doors that Jack himself would slam and lock for true crime writer Cameron Monroe. "Do you have it?"

Saura whipped the car around a curve. "In the backseat."

Camille glanced back, saw the laptop—and the portable printer. "You're a goddess," she said, and when Saura shot her one of those knowing smiles, something inside of Camille slipped quietly into place.

Older by a few years, Saura had always been more like a sister than a cousin. That was the way of it in big families. You had your siblings, but the bonds didn't stop there. You had cousins…and Camille had had Saura.

And she'd never forget the shock of opening her front door six weeks before and finding Saura. She'd tracked

Camille down, smiled a quirky little smile, then started to cry. Saura, her tough, gutsy cousin, had cried.

Time had plowed forward, but Saura still wore cutoff shorts that showed off her killer legs, and she still wore her long dark hair in a single braid down her back. But now a woman's wisdom shone in her dark eyes, a woman's loss—and a woman's love.

The rush of emotion surprised Camille. She'd gotten into the car that long-ago summer afternoon of her own volition, that was true. And when she'd reached New Orleans, where Saura had been waiting, she'd kept driving. She could have turned back. She could have called. But she'd never planned to stay gone.

She'd never planned a lot of things.

"What first?" Saura asked. "Pictures or sleuthing?"

And despite the thickness in her throat, Camille smiled. Looking at Saura Robichaud-soon-to-be-D'Ambrosia, no one would ever suspect she was one of the most successful, covert private detectives in New Orleans.

"Sleuthing," Camille said, sliding a pair of dark sunglasses over her eyes. She had a few bars to hit, a whole list of questions to ask. Starting with the actions of Jack's father the night he disappeared and ending with the drifter who'd come close to wiping out an entire family in his rush to avoid the authorities. If someone had seen him…maybe they'd seen who he was with. Or heard who he was talking to.

Then, later, in the privacy of Saura's car, where the all-seeing Sheriff Jacques Savoie would have no way of knowing, they could print the pictures Camille had taken of the map.

"I've got someone," Saura said, and Camille twisted around to see the beat-up pickup from the hotel ambling toward them.

Glancing at her cousin, she reached for the radio and cranked up the volume. "Then let's lose them."

"Find her."

"She's with her cousin—"

Standing in the waiting room, Jack swore quietly, but the nurses gathered around the station glanced up anyway. The younger grinned. The older…did not. "They could be halfway to New Orleans by now." If he was lucky. More likely, Camille and Saura were well on their way to trouble. He didn't for one second believe Russ lost them by accident. That had been Saura, adept at vanishing into shadows…even when there weren't any. "Keep looking."

"Roger that," Russ said. "That car sticks out around these parts. Finding them shouldn't be hard."

Jack bit back the hard sound that wanted to break from his throat. Russ meant well, but he didn't know the Robichauds. "Try Boudreau's." With the name of the bar came the memory. Both scraped. For years Jack had avoided the hole-in-the-wall, even as a teenager when sneaking into Boudreau's had been a coveted rite of passage. Except the once…

What the hell are you doing here?

She'd looked up at him with heavy-lidded bloodshot eyes, and smiled. *The better question is what are* you *doing here?*

Now, as sheriff, he routinely pushed through the doors of the last place his father had been seen alive. But never for the whiskey Gator had adored….

"I'll let you know," Russ was saying.

Jack ended the call and punched another series of numbers, frowned when he got Detective John D'Ambrosia's voice mail. "It's Jack," he said. "Seems your fiancée is playing *Thelma and Louise* again…."

Minutes passed. Russ didn't call. Jack crossed the small waiting room to the floral sofas, where Margot sat with Annie asleep in her lap. Little Greg stared at the cartoon on the television, while his father stared out the window.

"Mrs. Landry, can I get you something?" Jack asked. "Some water maybe?"

She smiled tightly and shook her head. "Only one thing I want right now, Sheriff, and only Dr. Graham can give me that."

Jack nodded. "I understand."

"Well I don't." This from Greg. Normally neat and tidy in a starched shirt, now his collar hung open and his tie lay draped around his neck like a broken noose. He strode toward them, prompting Jack to step back, out of the children's hearing.

He knew the look in the other man's eyes too damned well. "Greg—"

"A high-speed chase?" Janelle's husband bit the words out. "Here in Bayou d'Espere? What were your boys thinkin', Jack?" Not sheriff. "This isn't N'awlins. Janie and the kids could have been—" He broke off and paled, the unspoken word hanging there between them.

Killed. Janelle and the kids could have been killed. Just like—

"It has to do with her, doesn't it?" Greg asked, and the sheen in his eyes turned to accusation. "The Fontenot girl. I saw her there with you."

Jack held himself very still. "There was a break-in at Live Oak. A safe-deposit box was stolen."

"I know all that."

"The driver of the car that hit Janelle—"

"Was the man who broke into the savings and loan. I know that. But don't you just find it a little odd? The second Camille Fontenot shows her face in this town again, we have our first bank robbery in twenty-five years—and our first high-speed chase?"

Not odd.

It was exactly what Jack had feared. All his life there'd only been one thing, one person, he'd never been able to rein in.

And like the hurricane that had decimated the Gulf Coast almost fifty years before, her name was Camille.

Not much light remained. The sun dipped low against the western horizon, leaving blood-red streaks and swirls in its wake. The trees darkened into hulking shadows. The breeze, still warm, kept right on whispering.

"Maybe we should come back in the morning."

"No." With her hand to the car door, Camille turned toward her cousin. "I need to do this."

"Then let me go with you."

"No." The word came out harsher than Camille intended, so she softened it with a smile. "This is something I need to do."

Saura wasn't one to sigh or acquiesce, but she leaned back against the driver's seat and did just that. "I know," she said. And she did. More than most, Saura Robichaud knew about exorcising demons. "But I'm going to be right here," she said. "If you need me—"

"I will," Camille assured her. They'd spent the better part of the afternoon talking to locals about the conspiracy theories surrounding her father's death. Some folks had recognized Camille, welcomed her back. Others had recognized her, and shut down completely. Some hadn't made any connection at all.

After leaving the country grocery, Camille had climbed into the backseat and printed the pictures she'd taken of her father's map, while Saura had once again given the deputy the slip.

"You have everything?" she asked.

Their eyes met. Silently Camille flipped open her purse and revealed the handgun tucked inside. A Beretta. She'd picked it up several years before, when her research had made a killer a little too uncomfortable.

He'd been arrested two months later, but the gun had stayed.

With a slow smile, Camille ignored the pounding of her heart and pushed open the door. "Give me fifteen," she said, turning, and for the first time since the car had emerged from the heavily treed road leading to the house, Camille allowed herself to look.

It still stood. Surrounded by beautiful oaks and set back from the drive, the rustic two-story home that had been in her father's family for generations still stood. No one had lived there for years, but her mother had been unable to sell it—and Katrina had been unable to destroy it.

Both had tried.

Around Camille the familiar hymn of her childhood whispered on the breeze, the cicadas and the crickets, the toads. But the house was still, quiet. No dog bounded to greet her—and no laughter rang through the trees.

Her throat tightened, but she moved forward anyway, slipped her hand into her pocket and closed her fingers around the key her mother had given her.

Closure, she remembered saying. She wanted all those doors closed and locked…even if she had to walk through them first.

Three steps brought her to the veranda. Where petunias had once crowded clay pots, now shadows slipped and fell.

Slowly she turned. But there was nothing slow about all those little fissures inside her, the ones she'd damned up and walled away. They shattered the second she saw the old swing on the far side of the porch swaying with the breeze.

And the man sprawled against the seat.

Chapter 5

"Welcome home, *'tite chat*."

Her heart slammed hard, but for a moment everything else just…stopped. Sometimes he'd come to her like this, barge into the darkness of her dreams with an intensity that stole her breath. If she was being chased, it was Jack who stepped into her path and opened his arms. If she was hiding, it was Jack who reached for her, promised everything would be okay. And if she was making love—

If she was making love, it was Jack who wiped the tears from beneath her eyes, who held her hand and carried her into oblivion.

His movements were slow, almost lazy as he came to his feet, but the predatory stillness quickened through her. "Jack."

"Just like old times," he said quietly, but Camille recognized the deceptive tone. She'd heard it before. From cops. Sometimes lawyers.

But never Jacques.

Through the shadows he moved toward her, much the way he did in the darkness of her dreams. And even as she'd come home to prove nothing remained except those shadowy images that had her twisting in her sheets, part of her had wondered.

Part of her had wanted.

But as he closed in on her, his limp barely noticeable, the wondering ended. The years could be taken away, the goodbyes taken back. The mistakes could be fixed.

But this man, this tall, isolated man who'd been waiting for her in the darkness was not the boy who'd kissed her on the forehead all those years before.

"Cami!"

Saura's voice. Camille twisted toward her, saw her cousin hurrying toward her. But before Camille could call out a man stepped from behind a tree—and Saura froze. "Hang on there, Thelma."

"Tell her it's okay," Jack said. "Tell her she can go on home with her fiancé."

Her fiancé. The tall man dressed in black with whom Saura was having a heated conversation was her fiancé, Detective John D'Ambrosia.

"I'll take you home," Jack said. "You don't need her anymore."

The words swirled through Camille, slipped and slid against places she knew better than to allow them to touch. "I'm not hurting anything," she protested.

But Jack merely lounged against the door frame. "And I'm going to make sure no one hurts you."

"No one's going to hurt—"

"Finally, something we agree on."

This time the rush was softer and far, far more dangerous. She glanced toward her cousin, couldn't quite stop the smile that curved her mouth. "He called her Thelma?"

"Fits, wouldn't you say?"

It was the wrong time to laugh, but the sound slipped free anyway. "It's okay," she called to Saura. It took a little convincing, but finally Saura and D'Ambrosia headed toward the little black convertible. He reached for the keys, but she snatched her arm away and climbed into the driver's seat.

D'Ambrosia stalked to the other side.

"Wow," Camille murmured, but the second the red taillights vanished down the road, Jack was stepping closer, his lazy, good old boy act replaced by the hard-eyed cop from earlier that day. He took her by the elbow and turned her toward him, all but scorched her with the dark glow in his eyes.

"Mind telling me what you think you're doing?"

"You said it yourself," she said simply. "Coming home."

"Here," he shot back. "Alone."

"I wasn't alone."

The wide planes of his face tightened. "I could have been anyone, damn it. I could have been on you before—"

She twisted away. "But you *weren't*," she said. "You weren't just anyone, and you weren't on me." But the words, the image they brought, burned through her. "You're *Jack*," she said while the night pulsed around them, all those sounds and the muggy air, the breeze moving through the trees. "And you promised nothing would happen on your watch."

He stiffened. "Damn it, Camille—"

She stepped closer, stepped into him, stopped him with a finger to his mouth. "This isn't what I want," she said, but the words came out rough and hoarse and... broken. And again, the image taunted, of Jack...on top of her. All alone. In the darkness. With no one to hear or see...no one to know. "I don't want to be on opposite sides," she said, quieter this time. "I don't want to pretend—"

She broke off and looked beyond him, toward the empty porch swing.

"Pretend what?"

There was a note to his voice she didn't understand, an ache she'd not heard since she'd turned around to see him holding a gun on her. "Pretend you're the enemy."

Nothing prepared her for him to move. Nothing prepared her for him to lift a hand to her face and ease the hair behind her ear. "I'm not."

And with the words, something inside her shifted. "But you're not Jacques, either," she said. "When I look at you—" at his dark edgy eyes and the lines of his face, the hard mouth that had once been impossibly soft "—when you look at me...it's like the past isn't even there."

Except for then. It was there in that moment, glowing in his eyes like one of the candles on that long-ago night, when she'd wanted nothing more than for him to see she wasn't a little girl anymore—and she wasn't his sister.

"We can't live in the past, *cher.*"

The crickets still sang. She knew that. The cicadas and the toads, they were there. They always were. But Jack's words echoed through her, drowning out everything else.

"No," she said. "We can't."

* * *

Stillness breathed through the old house. Outside the glow of twilight had faded into night, leaving only darkness. She walked on anyway, moving from room to room as if not a day, a year, had passed.

Jack followed. He'd known she would show up here just as surely as he'd known he would be waiting. But the change rocked him. He'd come to expect secrets from her. He'd come to expect determination. During those dark years after her father's death she'd spun so far and dangerously out of control....

He'd tried to bring her back. Every time he'd looked at those desperate, devastated eyes, every time he'd heard the whispers, the allegations that his father had been the one to pull the trigger, that that's why Gator Savoie vanished...it had been like a knife twisting in his gut.

But in the end, the responsibility he'd felt for Camille had led him to violate a line that should never have been touched, much less crossed.

Now he watched her walk down the long hallway of her childhood, this woman she'd become, all grown-up with a woman's body and a woman's smile, the slow burn of a woman's eyes....

And the enormity of his mistake burned.

She wasn't a stranger. The girl was still there, buried beneath countless layers of scar tissue. She was still there...and she still ached for all she'd lost.

At the second to last room she hesitated, glanced back for a long heartbeat before stepping inside. And even before he followed, even before he lifted his flashlight, he knew the walls would be pale yellow, and that he'd find her crossing the matted carpet. On the far side she stopped and lifted a hand to the mural her mother had painted. It was a garden scene, Jack remembered, and Gloria Fontenot had immortalized Camille's kittens chasing a butterfly through daffodils.

"I'd forgotten," she whispered, and then she turned, exposing him to the saddest smile he'd ever seen. "I'd forgotten about the flowers."

He looked away.

"How does that happen, Jack? How do we just… forget?"

The question pierced.

The answer pierced deeper. People forgot, because they had to. People forgot, because remembering was too brutal.

"Time goes by," he said. "Things that aren't important just…fade."

Something dark and jagged flickered in her eyes. "But this *was* important. This room, these flowers…" She went down on her knees, and before she even lifted a hand, he directed the beam of light to the daffodils. "Sugar and Spice," she said, tracing the images of the two black-and-white kittens with her forefinger. Sugar had died young of undetected heart disease, but Spice…Spice had still been alive when Jack left for the Air Force. That would have made him six or seven.

"Mama still has him," she whispered, and Christ, through the shadows, he saw the moisture in her eyes. "And *he* remembered…" Her voice broke, and Jack couldn't do it one second longer, couldn't do nothing while she knelt on the floor of her childhood bedroom, and talked of the kitty who'd once slept against her chest.

He crossed to her, went down on one knee. "Camille…don't."

"He licked me," she said, somehow still smiling despite the tears in her eyes.

Jack's throat tightened. "Come on." He reached for her hand. "This was a bad idea—"

"No." She pulled back with a near violence that stunned him. "This is why I'm here…to remember."

He knew that. He knew she wanted to remember. For some crazy reason, she wanted to go back, to walk through those final days once again.

But the memories swimming in her eyes had nothing to do with the crime that had been committed at the other end of the house.

"Do you?" she asked. "Do you remember?"

He'd fought in two wars. He'd flown combat. He'd faced death—and buried a wife. Her question should not have twisted through him…should not have made him feel as if he stood on a sheet of very thin ice and the thaw was coming.

He thought about lying. That was the right thing to do. It was kinder, more merciful. *No.* He didn't remember. *Anything.* Because that's what he'd trained himself to do. That's what he'd demanded of himself. What he expected. The past was the past, and just like the furniture that had once occupied this house, it was gone now. Over.

But the house still stood, strong and sturdy, a place-holder against a world that tried to move on. Not even a category four hurricane had changed that.

"Yes." With the word he swiped at the tears beneath her eyes. "I remember."

Marcus says you kiss with your mouth open… That's not true, is it, Jacques?

She'd been seven or eight at the time, her hair in pigtails. Marcus had never talked to her of kissing again.

Teach me, Jacques...pleeeease. Teach me how to kiss....

She'd been sixteen then. Her father was dead. Crazy Cami, the kids at school had called her...sweet sixteen and never been kissed. Because no one wanted to kiss a freak.

He hurt me, Jacques.... Her lip had been swollen, bruised. Her eyes dark. Because he'd told her no. Jack had turned her down as gently as he could, told her he wasn't the one to teach her how to kiss. So she'd asked someone else. She'd asked Shawn Paul...and spinning on a six-pack of old Dixie, he'd been happy to oblige.

He hadn't been so happy after Gabe and Jacques got through with him.

Jack looked at her now, kneeling in the shadows with her hand on his knee, his hand still against her face. Her eyes were huge, dark, not with fear and pain, but a longing that fired through his blood.

"Jacques."

A stranger, he tried to tell himself. God, he wanted her to be a stranger. But her voice wrapped around his name the way it always had. Hero worship, Gabe had once called it.

But Jack was nobody's hero.

If he were, he would have pushed to his feet and taken her hand, led her out of that house, that place, led her back to New Orleans and deposited her with her mother. If he were, he would never have let her lean into him, would never have slid his hand to the back of her neck as she looked up at him...would never have crushed his mouth to hers.

Chapter 6

Teach me, Jacques…

He'd said no. He'd smiled gently and put his hands to her shoulders, pushed her back. She'd gone shopping that day. She'd gotten Saura to take her to a department store, had Saura pick out something trendy. Her jeans had been faded, her top black with a plunging neckline.

Jack hadn't even noticed.

He'd pushed her away, told her it wasn't his place. He'd turned then and walked away, gone back to Gabe's room, leaving Camille sitting on the edge of her bed…humiliated.

Over the years, she'd forgotten. She'd forgotten the way her body had burned, wanted. She'd forgotten how crushed she'd been the next day when she'd climbed up into the tree fort and found Jack and Lauralee sprawled on the floor, rolling around, kissing.

But here in this room, kneeling on the floor, the years

had fallen away, and she'd wanted again. When he touched her, when he put a hand to her face and wiped away her tears… Like the naive sixteen-year-old she'd been, she'd leaned into him.

But this time he didn't pull away.

His mouth moved against hers, soft and seeking, tentative kisses giving way to harder, deeper. In some foggy corner of her mind she was aware of the way he shifted and pulled her into his lap, the way his hand cradled her face, holding her, tenderly, gently, despite the urgency of his kiss.

Sensation swirled in a dizzying rush. Her breasts ached. Inside…she burned. She opened to him, went willingly as he lowered her to the ground and hovered over her. From the moment she'd walked into the old house, there'd been only cold. But now heat seeped from his body into hers. She could feel the strength of him, not refined and contained as she'd observed since coming home, but…broken, driven, needy in a way she'd never expected from the isolated man she'd come home to.

This, a little voice reminded. This was what she'd tried to blot from her mind. To erase. The way he'd kissed her that long-ago night before he'd left for active duty. She'd been…devastated. He was going away. He wouldn't be home for a long time, if ever. He was ending his life in Bayou d'Espere, finally getting away from the demons, the whispers that followed him everywhere.

Finally being the man his own father never was.

Camille had understood, and she'd tried to be happy for him. But she'd been unable to imagine life without him. She hadn't meant to seduce him that night. That's not why she'd brought the wine and the candles. She'd just wanted…

She didn't know what she'd wanted. She never had.

But Jack had come to Whispering Oaks as she'd asked. He'd found her, found the candles, had tried to leave.

To this day, she didn't know why he'd changed his mind. And to this day she didn't know how it had started, how the roles they'd always known had…shattered, leaving only the two of them and a clawing need that had carried them into the night.

It was the same desperation she tasted now, as if he wanted to absorb her. As if he *needed* to…

"Jacques…" She shifted against him, drinking in the feel of every hard line, the strength of his hands as they moved down her arms, his legs against hers, the ridge pressed against her thigh. She could feel—and she wanted. "Jacques."

And then it…stopped.

He ripped away with a violence that rocked her. His flashlight had fallen to the floor, leaving shadows to play against his face. His eyes were remote, shuttered, the line of his mouth hard, the whiskers at his jaw dark, the ones that had scraped so gently against the side of her face.

He might as well have driven a fist into her solar plexus.

"I'm sorry," he said, the way he had that morning, and part of her wanted to shove against him, to scream, to do something, anything, to destroy that wall of icy control that fell down around him. "Those aren't the memories you came home for."

Oh, but maybe they were. Sometimes memories destroyed, but sometimes they taught. And sometimes they strengthened.

With a quiet dignity she hadn't possessed when he'd left her kneeling on the floor, naked except for the quilt wrapped around her, she pushed to her feet and reached out a hand.

"No," she said, not the least bit surprised when he ignored her gesture and stood on his own. "They're not."

He retrieved his flashlight, jerked the beam away from the mural on the wall. "Come on," he said, heading toward the door. "We should—"

"No." With one last glance at the room she'd slept in for eighteen years, she turned and joined him in the hallway. "Not yet."

He'd been in Gabe's room. They'd been listening to the debut album of a new Irish rock band. Gabe had been sitting on the edge of his bed. He'd just broken up with his girlfriend. Jack had been on the floor, munching on the popcorn Camille had brought them.

The gunshot barely sounded above the lyrics.

I will follow...

But the scream had stopped his heart.

They'd been on their feet and running, racing through the darkness toward the scream that just kept echoing. And within seconds, they'd found her, Gabe's mom, kneeling in blood and draped over Gabe's father.

It had been obvious Mr. Troy was gone.

Jack watched her now, watched Camille kneel in the same spot her mother had. With mechanical move-ments—and absolutely no emotion—she ran her hand along the scarred hardwood floor, where the shattered remains of the stained glass had been found.

"I didn't hear the argument," she said, but he wasn't even sure she realized he was there. That kind of control, he'd seen it before. In combat. Soldiers were taught to suppress feeling, to shut it all out. That if they didn't, it could destroy.

"I didn't see the stained glass," she said. "I slipped in when they were fighting…"

The gun had gone off. Troy had fallen.

"Camille." He saw her flinch, saw her jerk. She twisted toward him, exposed him to eyes as horror-drenched as the morning he'd found her, two days later.

"No." Her voice was remote, controlled. "Not yet."

The sight of her reliving it all ripped through him. He knew better than to move, knew better than to touch, but something drove him to crouch beside her.

"You shouldn't be here," he said roughly. Sister, he told himself. She was Gabe's sister, for God's sake. Once she'd trusted him. "It can't be healthy—"

"It's not about healthy." Very little light leaked from the windows into the room, but her eyes glowed. "It's about unlocking doors," she said. "About coming to terms with what happened here."

"Closure." He realized.

Her answering smile surprised him. It was sad…reflective. "I've been running a long time," she acknowledged in that same quiet voice, the one that sounded grown-up and like a little girl all at the same time. "It's time to stop."

"And then what?" he asked, but did not let himself touch, not even to slide back the hair that had slipped from her ponytail and stuck against her mouth. "What happens when you stop?"

Her smile faded. She looked away, toward the windows, and stood. She crossed the room and lifted a hand to the pane. But she didn't say a word.

Somehow, he still heard.

She didn't know. She didn't know what would happen when she stopped.

But he did. He knew what happened when you stopped, when the stillness seeped in. The quiet. He knew what happened when the memories were scraped away and cataloged, when the past was laid to rest and the future stretched like a long road in front of you. He knew what happened when the dreams died and the nightmares went quiet. He knew what the silence sounded like.

"You don't need to do this," he said. Watching the way she stood without moving, looking into the backyard where the fort had stood, he crossed to her. She stiffened, but he put his hands to her shoulders anyway.

"Do what?" she asked.

"Make yourself remember." With the words, the truth formed. "Torture yourself." As some sort of misplaced penance. "To make up for your perceived sins…to do what you couldn't do before."

There was nowhere for her to go, captured as she was between his body and the window.

She took a step back anyway. "This isn't about penance."

"Isn't it? Are you sure? Because it sure seems that way to me. You were there, *'tite chat.*" The flare of her eyes touched him in ways he refused to let himself feel. "You were in the room. And you've always wondered, haven't you? You've always wondered what would have happened if you'd walked in a minute or two earlier? If you'd made your presence known."

Slowly, she shook her head.

"What if you'd screamed? You could have stopped them."

"No." The word was sharp…broken.

"So here you are now, ready to testify, to immerse yourself all over again, to go back and live that night again and again and—"

"He's lived like a king!" The words erupted from her as she came alive and shoved hard against his body.

But Jack didn't move, just kept standing there, sandwiching her between his body and the window.

"He acts like he owns the city," she hissed as Jack took her wrists and simply held her. "Do you have any idea what it was like, any idea at all, seeing him all these years? Seeing him on television, being treated like a celebrity…a god? Seeing him smile as he fakes his Cajun accent, seeing his face smirking at me from cookbooks? Everywhere I looked—"

"Then why now?" The question ate at him. "Why not before? Why wait all these years to make your move? You could have stopped—"

"No!" She twisted away, stared off into the darkness beyond the window.

Jack told himself to step away, that he'd pressed enough. But the cop he'd become joined with the boy he'd been—and for the first time since Camille had come home, he felt fear.

Hers.

"Hey…" The cop told him to give her space. The man he didn't want to be urged him to turn her in his arms and take her face in his hands, press his advantage.

But it was the boy who won, the boy who guided his hands around her waist. "Talk to me," he murmured. "Tell me…"

Everything. He wanted it all, every last detail. Why

she'd gone away—why she'd stayed away. Why she'd severed ties with her family. Why she'd let them worry that she could be dead when all the while she'd been watching from afar....

"The tree house is gone."

The words, so soft and out of the blue, slipped through him like an unexpected shot of whiskey. He looked through her reflection toward the sprawling old oak fifty feet from the house, where he and Gabe had once built a fort.

"Katrina," he told her. "She hit us hard."

Beneath his hands, Camille's shoulders, normally tense and squared, dropped. "I tried to find out," she said, and in her voice, he heard the same agony he'd felt halfway around the world. "For days I searched the Internet...went to the news sites, the television stations and newspapers...."

In those first few days, solid information had been impossible to come by. The images captured on film, those of entire neighborhoods under water, of citizens trapped and abandoned, had chilled.

"You were still there, weren't you?" she asked, and in the window's reflection, she lifted her eyes to his. "In the Middle East."

He closed his eyes, could still feel the sting of the sand. He'd been in Iraq. Well to the north of Baghdad, Kirkuk had been relatively secure. The insurgency had been in its infancy. But only two weeks before, a female pilot had been picked off while walking to get mail.

Jack's wife of eighteen months, Susan, had been in Louisiana.

"Yeah." The images slammed in from opposite directions, the ugliness of the war, and the destruction of his home. Maybe that's why he'd let the young children lull him into complacency a few weeks later. Maybe that's why he'd trusted…when he should have been alert.

Maybe that's why he'd damn near lost his leg—and had lost his career.

"I always knew it could happen," she said. "I remember Dad talking about the levees and that New Orleans was shaped like a bowl and if the big one ever hit, she'd go under."

His dad had predicted the same thing. But human nature was funny that way. Folks tended to wallow in horrible possibilities, but never really thought anything bad would happen. Not to them.

"I remember watching the cable news shows and seeing the satellite imagery, the track straight for New Orleans. And I remember…"

Her voice trailed off, and through the silence, another voice sounded. Susan's. She'd called him, terrified. She'd told him she was evacuating, that she wanted out, to go far. That she didn't want to be there anymore….

He should have let her go then. He should have realized how miserable she'd become, that being the wife of an airman was not the glamorous life she'd craved. That after the adrenaline rush faded, reality began. And that just because Jack could put on a flight suit and fly combat, that didn't mean there weren't skeletons in his closet. That there wasn't murder…secrets.

He'd been wrong to bring her to Louisiana. Wrong to think she'd be happy there.

"What?" he asked, dragging his mind away from Susan, and back to Camille. Without thought, his hand found his thigh.

"My friends didn't understand why I was uneasy. Folks in California didn't really understand how devastating the big one could be."

California. It was the first time she'd mentioned a place.

"No small irony there," he muttered.

Her smile was brief, fleeting. "No," she said. "Everyone loves to talk about the big one, that part of California will fall into the Pacific, but no one actually thinks it will happen."

Her words, so close to his thoughts moments before, had him drawing her closer.

For the first time, she didn't resist. "But I knew," she said. "I knew what would happen and when it did…"

"When it did, what, *'tite chat?*" He wanted to hear her say the words. *Needed* her to.

"I was half a country away, but…*I felt it,*" she whispered. "I felt it all…*everything.*"

He didn't want to believe her. He didn't want to think of her that way, thousands of miles away and hurting, worrying….

"I kept thinking about Bayou d'Espere," she whispered. "The trees and the beautiful houses, and I was terrified that I'd look up and find some reporter in one of those dumb boats making his way down Main Street, and that everything would be gone."

"Then why didn't you come back?" The question was low and hoarse. "Why didn't you try to help?"

"I couldn't."

She kept saying that. That she couldn't come back. That it wasn't that simple, that easy. "Why not?" Somehow he kept the accusation from his voice. "People were desperate for volunteers—"

She twisted and damn near slayed him with the glow in her eyes. "I bought a plane ticket. I had my bag packed—"

He gave her a second to finish. When she didn't, he lifted a hand to slide the hair from her face. Nice, he told himself. And. Slow.

But all those hard edges kept grinding away. "But what?"

"I kept calling Mama's house, Gabe's office, anywhere I could think of to get information."

But the lines had been down. He'd been trying, too.

"Then I ran across a news story about the courthouse, all the cases pending trial…and he was there." She moistened her lips before continuing. "Gabe was. He was quoted," she said.

Jack remembered the story—he'd seen it himself. It had run on one of the cable news networks. The air had damn near burst out of Jack's chest when he'd seen Gabe's tired, shadowed face on the television.

"He talked about how he'd gotten his family to safety," she said, "but then he'd gone back to the courthouse with the D.A. and a few of the other A.D.A.'s, to keep things safe."

Jack let out a rough breath. "So you decided you weren't needed after all."

The stillness was immediate, in her body, her eyes. "It wasn't a question of being needed."

"Then what?" Secrets screamed from every tight line of her body—a woman's body that the girl had not possessed.

He wanted…the secrets. He wanted the secrets. "What *was* it a question—"

The sound of a floorboard creaking killed his words. He spun, reached for his gun.

"Jack—"

He pulled her away from the window and positioned her against the wall. "Stay here."

"No, don't go—"

"I'll be back," he promised, already running. Someone had been inside. Someone had been crouched in the darkness, listening. Waiting.

At the door, he grabbed the knob and turned the small lock, pulled it shut behind him and ran toward the front of the house.

She counted to ten. That was the only head start she would give him. By eight the sound of his footsteps had fallen silent. By nine, the front door had slammed shut.

By ten, there was nothing.

She broke from the wall and ran through the darkness, complete now, a total blackout. Jack had taken his flashlight, but she didn't need it. The room stood empty. The door was just across—

Her foot slammed into something solid and unmovable.

She staggered and flung out her arms, went down hard. She tried to catch herself with her hands, but her wrist twisted, leaving the impact with the hardwood floor to sing through her bones. For a moment she sprawled on the floor of her father's study in much the same place that she'd once seen him go down, and tried to breathe.

"Cami."

The voice slipped through the stillness, and stopped her cold.

"Camille Rose."

Her heart kicked. The voice…it was low and raspy, and through the darkness of her mind, something stirred.

"It's been a long time, sweet girl."

Sweet girl. The nickname speared deep, sent the room into a hard tilt. Only one man had ever called her sweet girl....

"Daddy..." The word slipped past the horror. She heard her voice break, could do nothing about the way her throat closed up.

"That's my girl," he said. "Easy does it."

The spinning intensified, whirling, blurring. Faster. Crueler. Harder. She fought it, fought the vertigo, the memory, somehow pulled herself to her knees, forced a breath. "Who are you?" she demanded.

Not her father, she knew. Not. Her. Father.

"You know who I am," he whispered. "You've always known."

She blinked hard, told herself it wasn't real. He wasn't real. Wasn't there. She was alone. Jack would—

The light blinded her. It came on without warning and shot across the room, locked on her like the beam of a searchlight. "Still so damned pretty..."

That voice. She knew that voice, had heard it....

No. Denial streaked through her.

No.

He'd been in the room the whole time. He'd been in there when she and Jack had stood at the window, when they'd talked about Katrina. The man who now held the flashlight on her had made the noise deliberately to lure Jack away from her.

"What do you want?" she demanded, and then she refused to kneel there like some trapped animal one second longer. She brought herself to her feet, lifted her chin. "Jack will be back—"

"You know what I want," the man said. "You've always known."

She wanted to back away. She wanted to charge forward. But she allowed herself neither. Not when the glare of the light blinded her. Not when she didn't know exactly where he stood, or if he had a gun. "The map." There was absolutely no emotion to her voice. "You want my father's map."

"Always such a good girl. I knew you'd come back someday."

The memory stabbed—the photographs on the table depicting her mother's car. She'd been driving down Canal Street. It had been dusk. The light had been green.

Gloria Fontenot had never seen the car barreling down Rampart...

The accident scene. Camille's mother sprawled against the front seat of the car. The blood. The paramedics running toward the demolished car. Her mother on the gurney—in the hospital. All a not-so-subtle warning for Camille to stay away.

"You son of a bitch!" she hissed now, as she'd been unable to do all those years ago, when fear had paralyzed her, made her weak even as she tried to be strong.

She'd never realized that in playing his game, she'd all but handed Marcel Lambert sure victory.

"Shoot me!" she dared, and this time she moved, took a long step toward him. "Go ahead, do it. Shoot me."

His laughter was soft. "You know that's not what I want."

"You don't scare me," she said with another step, and then she smelled it, the trace of cigarette smoke—and the whiskey.

Just like that night so long ago.

"Because you can't hurt me," she said. "And we both know it. If you do—"

"Camille!"

The voice slammed into her, had her spinning toward the door. "Jack! Don't—" But it was too late. The loud crash broke through the darkness and he was there, charging into the room.

"I have a gun!" he shouted.

Then a grunt, a thud. Footsteps racing from the room. Silence within.

Camille lunged and dropped to her knees, reached for Jack, until she found him sprawled just inside the door. "Jack. My God—"

"Maudit fils de putain!" In one svelte move he was on his knees and running his hands along her body. "Sweet Mary, are you okay? Did he touch you? What the hell—"

"I'm fine." She kept her voice steady, even as part of her started to shake. "He didn't touch me."

But Jack did. Jack touched her, slid his hands along her arms to her neck, her face. He held her there, his hands against her cheeks, and even without light, she could see the primal gleam in his eyes.

"It was a trick," she said. "He wanted me alone… thought he could scare me."

"Who?"

She swallowed hard, knew she had to tell him. "The man from that night," she said. "The one who chased me."

For a moment silence screamed between them, stillness, as they kneeled a heartbeat from each other in the darkness of her father's study. The warmth of Jack's breath feathered over her, the erratic riff of his heart punished.

"He was here," Jack finally repeated, and the words were cold and furious, brutal.

Maybe it was the edge to his voice, the way he'd charged in without one clue what he would find. Or maybe it was the lingering echo of the thud, that moment when she knew he'd gone down.

Or the fact he'd stayed with her, he'd reached for her, made sure she was okay…while Marcel Lambert got away.

It could have been any of those things, or none of those things. But in the end it didn't matter. In the end there was just her and Jacques, again, and she lifted her hands to his.

"He wanted the map," she whispered.

Jack swore lowly and creatively, purely in Cajun. And all that cold she'd been fighting for longer than she cared to remember, started to slip away.

"Kinda makes you wonder why, doesn't it?" About the map—and the warmth. "If that stained glass window really broke…why is Lambert so hot to get his hands on my dad's map?"

Around them, the stillness extended. Even the cicadas had fallen quiet. "He's not going to win," Jack muttered. "So help me God that bastard is not going to win."

"No," Camille said. "He's not. That's why I'm here, Jack." That's why she had to write the book.

He pulled his hands from beneath hers without warning, and stood. "Come on."

Through the shadows, she saw him reach for her. From the moment she'd decided to write *Sins of the Storm*, she'd known this man, Jacques Savoie—not Marcel Lambert—would be her biggest challenge. She'd known how easy it would be to slip into roles of the past, she the adoring little girl hanging on his every word. She'd known, and she'd prepared.

But now all those plans crumbled, and she put her hand in his and let him help her to her feet.

The wince just kind of happened. It was dark, there was no reason he should have seen it, no reason he should have known. But he was there anyway, sliding an arm around her waist. "You're hurt—"

"No," she managed. "Just my wrist…"

On a low oath he loosened his grip on her hand. "What kind of a sick bastard—" he started, but did not finish. Because they both knew. "He's not going to get to you again," Jack promised, heading toward the door. "Not without going through me first."

Chapter 7

The cozy Acadian house, set back from the road and sur-rounded by pine and cypress, didn't surprise her. Jack had grown up in a trailer. His father had talked about building a house for his family, had even drawn up plans. Jack had shown them to her and Gabe...sometimes the three of them had trekked through the woods looking for the right spot.

But then, after the night a single bullet shattered too many lives, she'd never heard Jack mention the house in the woods again.

She'd never heard him mention his father, either.

It was as if that boy and that man had simply ceased to exist.

Until now. She paced the sprawling main room, with its distressed hardwood floor and paneled walls, large windows overlooking the wide porch, the woods farther back. Beyond them, hidden by the darkness, a lake.

But inside…not much.

A man's house, she told herself. Jack was a bachelor. He lived alone. She wouldn't expect curtains. She wouldn't expect rugs and throw pillows, candlesticks on the mantel or coasters on the coffee table. But somehow their absence…

Their absence was wrong. Jack had brought a wife with him to Bayou d'Espere, and even if she was gone now, there should be some remnant, some lingering whisper of the life they'd been building together.

The piano made Camille smile. It had been Jack's grandmother's. The fiddle mounted above, his grandfather's. As kids she and Gabe had sometimes gone to their house on Christmas Eve, listened to the elder Savoies play their instruments and sing carols. Jack had been learning to play the fiddle when his grandfather passed.

Throat tight, Camille ran her finger along the top of the piano, where most people would have placed photos or other memorabilia, maybe a metronome.

But her fingers encountered only dust.

Turning, she wandered to the sofa and flipped through the newspaper tossed on the trunk that served as a coffee table—and saw the book.

Secret Sins.

The title glared up at her. Just below, she saw the name of the woman she'd worked hard to become, Cameron Monroe. She picked the paperback up, could tell it was new.

And dread settled like a heavy weight against her chest.

"Here you go."

She spun toward the voice, saw him emerging from the kitchen with two mugs in one hand, first-aid supplies in the other, and a slightly more pronounced hitch to his gait. He'd barely spoken since leaving her childhood home, had spent most of his time on the phone with Detective D'Ambrosia and Russ. Since he'd led her inside there'd been nothing other than a clipped "wait here."

Now Jack strode toward her, all six foot two of him, in the same faded jeans he'd been wearing all day. His shirt was black, a button-down open at the throat with the sleeves rolled up, a tear at the bicep and below the left breast pocket. His dark brown hair fell against the cowlick at the center of his forehead…and revealed the gash at his temple.

"Drink up," he said.

She took the mug and brought it to her mouth, but when she sipped, it was not chocolate that made her senses hum. "Trying to knock me out?" she asked, half smiling, half accusing, but Jack had already turned away. She took another sip, this time savored the slow burn of whiskey.

"You better let me have a look at that," she said.

He set the peroxide and cotton balls on the trunk. "Look at what?"

"Your forehead…he gashed you pretty good."

His hand came up to finger the wound. "Just the surface."

"All the same—"

"Camille." Only her name, that was all he said, but the sound of it on his voice did cruel things to her heart. It strummed low and sent a dangerous heat whispering through her blood.

It was the first time in years he'd spoken her name in anything other than anger or frustration. Or regret.

"Jacques." Her own voice thickened on his name, and when she looked into his eyes, the agitation in those dark chocolate depths knocked the breath from her lungs. "You're hurt—"

Like a curtain falling, the slow wash of emotion vanished, replaced by a steeliness that chilled.

"This isn't about me," he said, moving toward her. But he did not reach for her, did not touch. "This is about you, and Marcel Lambert, and a game that is not going to have a happy ending."

Happy ending. The words lanced through her.

"He doesn't scare me," she said with another sip of the laced cocoa. "He's desperate, grasping at straws." Because for the first time, little Cami Rose was not playing by his rules. "If he'd wanted to hurt me—"

"He did hurt you, damn it!" Now he touched. He put his hands to her shoulders and dragged her so close she could see that he was right, that the wound at his temple was little more than a bruise—much like the scrapes on her knees.

"He hurt you then, and he hurt you tonight, and *maudit* I'm not going to let him do it again!"

Everything inside her stilled. She looked up at him, at his wide cheekbones and the whiskers darkening his jaw, and felt something inside of her shatter.

That's why she stepped back. When all those broken edges inside collided with each other, and the memories poured free.

"You blame yourself, don't you?" The question was barely more than a whisper. "You blame yourself for what happened."

His eyes darkened. "I'm a cop. I should have recognized the trap. I should have—"

"Not tonight," she said. "But then, all those years ago, when we made love."

The words, bottled up for so long, stung on the way out.

Jack stood so very still, the mug still in his hand, a mug, she would guess, that contained far more whiskey than cocoa.

"You blame yourself for taking advantage of me." She pushed—even though if anyone had taken anything, advantage or otherwise, it had been her. She'd just wanted.

God, she'd wanted so much.

"For hurting me," she said. "You think that's why I left." It had been to get away, *to breathe.* But only at first. "For stealing my happy ending."

She saw his throat work, his eyes burn.

"And for her, too, don't you?" she went on, not sure where the insight came from, not sure why she kept prodding when any smart rational woman could see that Jacques Savoie was not an animal who enjoyed having his back against the wall. "Your wife."

His nostrils flared. "Don't psychoanalyze me."

She gestured toward the old piano, the mantel, where a wedding picture should have sat. "Then where is she? Where is your wife?" The word hurt. "Why isn't she here?"

He didn't look to where she pointed, just kept his eyes on hers. "She's dead."

There was absolutely no emotion to his voice. "I know that," she said, softer this time. Her mother had told her about the accident, the horrible speculation that Susan Savoie had been drinking—just like Jack's father. "But you're not."

The second the words left her mouth, she realized her mistake.

Jacques Savoie, the son of the town drunk, a boy who'd left behind his childhood to chase his own dreams, who'd gone to war and almost lost his leg, who'd returned to find the land of his birth ransacked by Mother Nature, who'd been driving home one night when he'd seen the car wrapped around a tree—and found his wife thrown twisted in the wreckage. He stood here now with a glitter in his eyes…but inside, he was as dead as everyone he'd buried.

"It wasn't your fault." She moved before she could talk herself out of it. She crossed to him and took the mug from his hands, set it on the trunk. "None of it." The need to comfort, help him out of the dark place into which he'd retreated, drove her. She reached for him—

He stiffened. "You don't want to touch me right now."

The words, a cold, seductive gauntlet, stopped her. "Why not? You might do something we'd both regret?"

"You have no idea what I'm capable of."

"Don't be so sure of that." The quickening started low, spread fast. "This is me, Jack. *Me.* Cami. Camille Rose. You can pretend I'm a stranger all you like. You can pretend I don't know you, that I don't *understand.*" Heart slamming, she took one slow step toward him. "Because God knows it would be easier that way, wouldn't it? But inside you know the truth. We both do. No matter what happened that night at Whispering Oaks—" when a bottle of wine had transformed an emotional goodbye into a life-changing mistake "—no matter what happened in Iraq, *with your wife*…nothing can change who I am to you. Or what I know."

That somewhere deep inside, he was still Gator's son, whose life had spun so horribly out of control despite how tightly he'd held on.

Slowly, as he did almost everything, with that exquisite, almost terrifying deliberation, he stepped toward her. "You think I want you to be someone else?" The question was so soft she had to concentrate to make out the words. "Is that what you think this is about? That I won't let myself see you?"

She tried to swallow, found her throat dry. "It's kind of hard to think anything else."

"Is that what you want?" he asked. "Is that what this is all about, the way you sneaked back into town without so much as an e-mail to let me know you were going to be here? Isn't that what *you're* doing? Trying to pretend the past isn't there…that you're not still that wild child desperate for someone to pay attention to her…that I'm not—"

The glitter in his eyes went out. And some crazy little voice warned her to back away.

But an even crazier voice dared her to stay exactly where she was.

"What?" she asked against the tight band of emotion. "Not the what?"

"Because we can sure do that." He rolled on in that same low quiet voice, as if she'd said nothing, asked nothing. "It sure would be more fun that way, wouldn't it?"

If his expression hadn't been so blank, the words would have slipped clear to her soul.

"We can pretend there's absolutely nothing there…."

Strangers. With no past, no regrets. No guilt. No ties, no connections. Only the slow curl of heat. "Can we?"

"We can do anything you want." His eyes took on a languorous burn. "As long as you're sure that's really the game you want to play…."

The rhythm of her heart changed, deepened. "Jack—"

"Because trust me, if that were the case, if we were really strangers...we sure wouldn't be standing here right now."

All these years. All these years she'd worked to carve this man from her memory, to think of him only as a boy, a childhood crush—to ignore the influence he'd wielded over her. She'd tried not to think of the man he would have grown into—and the damage that might have been done along the way.

But here, now, standing in his utilitarian living room in the little house in the woods, with the fronts of her legs brushing his jeans, she realized the man—with his man's eyes and man's hurt, his man's dare—was far more lethal than the boy.

"And I sure as hell wouldn't be worried about from which direction Lambert is going to attack next."

Words. That's all they were. Soft, stealthy. But they wove through her.

"We'd be in my bed," he said, and this time he put his hand to her chin and tilted her face to his. "Naked."

Everything stilled. She tried to piece it all together, to draw the line from point A to point B. She'd challenged him about his wife, the past. She'd tried to make him see none of it was his fault.

But somehow he'd twisted the conversation. He'd stepped off the defensive, and gone on the prowl. Because she was too close, she realized. She'd slipped too close to the place he kept walled away. Even from himself.

Especially from himself.

"You think so?" Her mouth curved. "That's a mighty big assumption considering it takes two—"

"My point exactly." Watching her, his eyes so hot she

instinctively swallowed, he stroked his thumb along her lower lip. "If you didn't know me…if the past wasn't there…there'd be no reason to say no."

The quiet words, so excruciatingly true, jammed the breath in her throat.

"But Cami knows," he said, and his smile was no longer predatory, but oddly gentle. "Cami Rose has always known."

She refused to step back.

"I see you, *Camille*," he drawled, letting his hand fall from her face. "And trust me, I know exactly who you are."

And he didn't sound the least bit pleased about it.

It was an odd time to smile, but she did anyway. "Keep telling yourself that, Sheriff…and one of these days you just might believe it."

The night deepened. Off in the distance heat lightning flickered across the horizon, but no thunder followed, and no rain would come.

Jack stood at the edge of the porch with his hands around the rail, and waited. At his feet, his big yellow Lab watched intently. Beauregard's tail swished. His eyes glowed. In his mouth he held a slobbery, chewed-up yellow Frisbee. But Jack had played enough. Any minute headlights would cut through the darkness. His deputy had called shortly before eleven. And while Russ Melancon was a rookie, not yet twenty-five, the kid had the composure of a veteran.

But for the second time that day, he'd sounded…shaken.

From the oaks surrounding the house, the cicadas kept a steady rhythm. They would let him know when Russ drew close. They let him know everything.

Susan had hated the cicadas.

Within minutes their rhythm intensified, and like clockwork, the glow of headlights cut into the darkness.

All the while, inside, Camille slept.

Jack pushed the thought aside, didn't want to think of her curled between the sheets of his guest bed in that oversize T-shirt he'd found her wearing that morning.

Instead he waited while Russ parked his squad car then strode toward the house.

"Got it, Sheriff," he said, hurrying up the three steps that led to the porch. "I got the laptop."

Through the yellow glow of the light, Jack noted the black briefcase, sleek. Stylish. It alone would set someone back a nice penny. "Camille's?"

"Found a hotel receipt in Hebert's wallet," Russ said. "Down in Lafourche Parish. I went over and talked to the manager…found this in the Dumpster out back."

Something quick and potent licked through Jack. The man who'd broken into the savings and loan had ditched the computer. That either meant there was nothing else of value on the hard drive…or he'd found what he wanted and didn't want to get caught with the evidence.

Camille had been unwilling to confirm either theory.

Jack took the satchel and flipped it open, pulled out the laptop. New, he noted, sliding his index finger to the power button. Small, state-of-the-art.

"Um…how well do you know this Fontenot woman, Sheriff?"

The question stopped Jack cold. He looked up from the computer language flashing across the screen, to find his deputy watching him with the same hesitation that had weakened his voice. "Better than she knows herself."

That was the problem.

Camille Fontenot tore through life with the same reckless disregard as her namesake. He'd hoped with time she'd find peace, closure.

But if anything, the years away from Bayou d'Espere had pushed her closer to the edge.

"Oh," Russ said. "Then you already know."

Jack felt a small muscle in the hollow of his cheek thump. "Know what?"

His deputy strolled over and clicked open the word processing program, pulled up a file. "I'm just glad she's here with you, Sheriff."

Four words appeared against the stark white of the screen—black, bold, all caps.

"Cuz if Billy Hebert is on Marcel Lambert's payroll…"

Everything inside of Jack went cold. Russ still talked. Jack knew that. Beauregard nudged at his hand—and the cicadas screamed. But the low roar of his blood drumming against his ears drowned out everything…except those four simple words.

One night. One bullet. One gunshot. But with it more than just one man fell. More than just one man died. Families collapsed, and childhoods ended. Innocence shattered, and a dark dance of lies and betrayal began.

Jack stared at the computer screen, didn't trust himself to move. Russ stood a few feet across the porch, pretending to roughhouse with Beauregard. But Jack knew his deputy watched. He could feel the burn of his gaze, the questions. The…curiosity.

It was all there, on the computer, in file after file. Her secrets, her thoughts and memories and plans. *Her agenda.*

The word, the reality, settled like a rock in his gut.

He'd known she had secrets. He'd seen them crowding her eyes. He'd known there was something she wasn't telling him. She'd been too driven. Too...deliberate.

But God Christ have mercy, he'd never imagined—

God Christ have mercy, Camille hadn't come home because she was curious about her father's safe-deposit box, or to testify against Marcel Lambert.

She'd come home to crucify him.

As Cameron Monroe.

Jack looked up toward the night, refused to let himself look toward the house, where she slept inside, so goddamned innocently. She. Camille—Cameron Monroe. The author preparing to serve up every prurient detail, every crumb about her own father's death for public consumption.

That's why she was here. That's why she'd come home. That's why she'd been at Whispering Oaks. That's why she'd sugared up to locals all afternoon, in bar after bar, after bar.

That's why she'd sidestepped his questions.

One night. One bullet. One gunshot.

Troy Fontenot was the victim's name. He was a husband and a father, a scholar. A dreamer. He was always home from work by six, washed the dishes after dinner, helped his son with his homework and read stories to his little girl. But after the house fell quiet Troy would retreat to his study, and there he would let his own passion take over.

Jack's cell phone started to ring.

It was that passion that drove him, controlled him…that passion that killed him.

The cicadas fell quiet.

That passion that killed them all—the families and the childhoods, that—

Jack looked up and reached for his phone, brought it to his face. "Savoie."

"Jacques."

Cold punched in from all directions. The voice was tired and frail and…scared, and before he even asked the question, he knew. "Gran? What's wrong?"

"I—I think someone's trying to get in," she said, but Jack was already running.

—killed the innocence.

The slam of a door broke her sleep. The rush of heavy footfalls jump-started her heart. And then his hands were on her body, curving around her, pulling her from beneath the covers. "Jacques—"

"Come on," he said, and before she could so much as breathe, she was on her feet and he was practically dragging her toward the door.

She blinked against the glare of light and tried to orient herself, staggered and slammed into him…felt the gun. "My God…" she tried, but her throat closed up on her,

and panic came in a tight cold fist. She caught sight of
him then, the tight lines of his face and the hot burn in
his eyes, and deep in her bones, she knew. "W-what's
going on?"

"There's no time—"

"Sheriff," came a second voice, "I can stay with her
if you like—"

"I'm not leaving her here."

Again.

He didn't say the word, but it echoed through the
silence. He'd left her earlier. He'd left her, and Lambert
had gotten to her.

Now he lifted her into his arms and continued toward
the front of the house. Without letting her get dressed.
Without even waiting for her to put on shoes.

With a gun.

"Follow me," he called back to the young deputy.
"Hank should already be there."

Camille reached for his arm, held on tight. "Where?"

He pushed open the front door and ran. "Gran's."

Russ stood at the window. Hank stood at the front
door. Another deputy stood just inside the kitchen. The
cozy little parlor, with its chintz drapery and chintz sofa,
the thick Aubusson rug, the antique buffet crowded by
picture frames, was completely surrounded. No one was
getting in without going through Jack's men first.

Outside on the porch, Detective D'Ambrosia waited.
Through the thick sheers he appeared more shadow than
man, but Camille watched him, watched the stillness. The
intensity. The way he stood with his gun in his hand,
without even seeming to breathe. Saura's fiancé had

arrived within minutes of Jack. The two had conferred, then Jack had taken off.

Now silence breathed through the old-fashioned room. Camille sat on the edge of the sofa, couldn't stop looking at the pictures. They were all there, all the photographs that were not at Jack's house. Of his mother and father, his grandparents. Of her and Gabe and Saura…of Jack in high school football pads. Him in a flight suit standing next to an F-16.

Of Jack in his dress blues…standing next to a dark-haired woman in a wispy white dress.

The urge to stand and step closer tugged at Camille, but she remained on the sofa, didn't let herself move.

"Are y'all sure I can't get y'all something?"

Camille glanced from the haunting photo toward the hot pink, velveteen wingback chair where Ruby Rose sat. With her parchment-thin hands clasped and her almost-shocking-blue eyes bright, Grandma Ruby looked from Russ to Hank, back to Russ. "Maybe some tea or coffee?"

"No, ma'am," Russ said.

Then Hank spoke up: "You just stay right where you are…that's what Jack said."

She frowned. "It was just that ole 'coon. I let my imagination git the better of me is all."

"Maybe," Russ said. "But until the sheriff gives the all clear, we need to be careful."

"I'm sure he'll be back in a few minutes," Camille said. She slipped from the camelback sofa and went to Jack's grandmother. "You know Jack. He's being careful."

Ruby Rose sighed. "Just look at you," she said, reaching for Camille. "All grown-up and still as pretty as can be."

She went down on her knees and took Grandma Ruby's hand, felt something soft and gentle shift through her. Jack's grandmother had to be pushing eighty, but she could easily pass for a woman ten years younger. Her skin was buttery soft, her coiffed hair still the color of cola...now no doubt courtesy of her sister Rita, who ran the local beauty shop. Her pajamas were silky—and straight from the pages of a well-known lingerie catalog. And the fuzzy fuchsia slippers on her feet...well, Camille was pretty sure they were intended for coeds in a dormitory.

"This is just such a surprise," she said. "I had no idea you were back."

"No one did."

The deceptively quiet voice swirled through Camille like the leading gust of a late-night storm. She twisted and saw Jack, instinctively reached for the edge of the chair. There was a stillness to him that chilled, the way he dominated the elegant foyer, his feet shoulder-width apart, his eyes unreadable. "Seems she's still not a big fan of radar."

The innuendo stung. Camille pushed to her feet and started toward him, acutely aware of the hardwood beneath her bare feet and the swirl of air-conditioning against her legs—Jack hadn't even given her time to dress.

No way was she going to give *him* advance warning— or Marcel Lambert time to evacuate.

No way was she going to give either of them time to take control.

"Did you find anything?" she asked, glancing from him to D'Ambrosia, who now stood inside the door.

Jack moved past her to his grandmother, took her hands in his. "Everything looks fine, Gran. I don't see any sign of attempted forced entry."

Grandma Ruby's smile was tired. "I feel so silly—"

"No." He brought a hand to her face. "You did the right thing. After the fire…"

Camille bit down on her lip but couldn't look away from the silent communion between Jack and his father's mother. She'd been widowed early, much like Jack's mother. Camille was willing to bet Jack still mowed her lawn and cleaned her gutters.

He always had.

And she could only imagine the horror of the fire that had gutted the vacant house two doors down a few months before. Arson, Saura had told her. The wind had thrown sparks toward Grandma Ruby's house, but the firefighters had intervened.

Then tonight, to get the phone call that his grandmother thought someone was outside…

Something sharp and cold cut through Camille. It wasn't coincidence. It was the hallmark of Marcel Lambert, the nasty mind games he got off on playing. Even while awaiting trial.

"But it's all safe now," Jack said with his back to Camille. He hadn't looked at her, spoken to her, since he'd deposited her in his car. "Why don't you go back on up to bed? Russ and Hank will stay here just to be sure."

Grandma Ruby stepped back from his arms. "That's not necessary—"

"Mais, grandmère," he said, and now his voice was thick, warm, and deep inside, Camille tensed. She knew that voice…had gone to superhuman lengths to scrub it from her memory. "It'll make me feel better all the same."

And with that, the battle was over. Ruby Rose had a will of iron, but a soft spot for her grandson a mile wide. Once he made it personal, once he made it about *him*, about making *him* feel better, the steel faded from her eyes, and her mouth curved. "*Mais oui,* if it'll help you sleep better…"

And that, Camille knew, was the danger of Jacques Savoie.

Darkness spilled around them. Silence breathed. She stepped from the squad car onto the gravel that comprised Jack's driveway, then crossed the cool damp grass to the front porch. Jack followed.

At the door, he pulled open the screen and put in his key, pushed inside and deactivated the alarm. Held the door. Let her in, let Beauregard out. Locked up behind them. Jabbed a series of buttons against the security panel.

Said nothing.

Just as he hadn't looked at her, touched her.

Slowly she turned toward him—but there was nothing slow about the way her breath caught. He stood next to a small marble-top table containing a lamp and not much else. His eyes were shuttered, his temple bruised. And in his hand, he still held the gun.

"Jack—"

"Go on to bed, Cam—" He stopped abruptly—unnaturally. And a hard sound broke from his throat. "*Camille.*"

Something about the way he said her name made her go very still. She saw the way he watched her as if she were a suspect…with nowhere to run.

And before he said anything else, before he flicked on the lamp…she knew. "Or would you rather me call you Cameron?"

Chapter 8

She'd chosen the name carefully. Cameron was a parish in southwestern Louisiana. In 1957 a hurricane named Audrey barreled ashore with little warning and wiped out everything in her path. Cameron was flattened. Four hundred and twenty-five people were killed. Of those, one hundred and fifty-four were under nine years old.

But out of that devastation emerged courage and grit and determination, and the community rebuilt. Cameron persevered. Cameron endured.

When Camille's editor asked about a pseudonym, Camille had thought about Audrey…and Cameron. As it was her parents had named her after a storm…but Camille didn't want a name that symbolized devastation. There'd been enough of that. She wanted…rebirth.

And Cameron Monroe was born.

She'd always found great satisfaction in the name,

even if no one other than she understood the symbolism. But here, now, standing in the shadows of Jack's living room, the acrid edge to his voice sent something dark and cold slipping through her.

She'd always known he would find out. She'd always known this moment would come. But she'd wanted it on her terms, at a time and a place of her choosing. Not… like this.

"Well, congratulations, Sheriff. Guess you don't need a radar screen, after all."

Whiskers had crowded his jaw since he'd found her at Whispering Oaks. That first night they'd invited her caress. Now, they warned her to stand back. "Trust me, *cher,* you don't want to know what I need."

She laughed. It wasn't the time or the place, but she wasn't about to fall for the blatant attempt at intimidation. "Oh, but there's a difference between wanting and knowing," she said in that same slow, deliberate tone he so preferred. "Maybe I don't want to know, but trust me, I do all the same."

He stepped toward her, stopped so close she couldn't so much as breathe without taking the scent of him— leather and soap and man—deep inside. "Then why don't you tell me."

The urge to retreat streaked through her, but with her calves against the sofa, there was nowhere to go. "It's not going to work," she said, even as her lungs forgot how to work. "You can try this big bad sheriff routine all you like, but I have nothing to apologize for."

He took another step. "Really?" His voice was hoarse, quiet. "Then maybe you should go on down to the hospital and tell that to Greg and his kids."

She stiffened.

"Or maybe you'd like to see Janelle herself—"

"I had no way of knowing—"

"Didn't you?" He pushed on in that same awful voice. "Isn't that why you didn't say anything. Not even to me?"

"Tell me something," she snapped, and all those broken edges, the ones she'd bandaged and protected for too many years, broke free. He stood so rigid and un-yielding, as if she'd known this horrific accident would happen, and pressed forward anyway.

"What difference would it have made? If I'd called? If I'd put myself on your sacred little radar screen?" The question tore from some wounded place inside. "Would you have met me at the airport? Would you have taken me to the bank, opened the safe-deposit box yourself?"

The muscle in the hollow of his cheek thumped. "I would have taken precautions," he said. "And yes, I would have taken you to get the safe-deposit box before anyone had a chance to steal your laptop."

And tip the terrible chain of events into motion.

"There would have been no high-speed chase." He pressed on with that same unnatural stillness. She tried to put some space between them, but the sofa made that im-possible. "No one would have gotten hurt," he said. "No one would have lured me away from you tonight." He paused, let a beat of silence throb between them. "And no one would be playing mind games with my grandmother."

Camille looked down, not wanting him to be right. "But why? This has nothing to do with her."

"A message," Jack said. "To me. And to you. That he's here, that he knows. That he can get to us, get to her— get to anyone."

Slowly, she looked up. "Because of my computer…"

The light in Jack's eyes went dark. He reached around her and picked up something from the sofa, pulled his arm back to reveal the laptop. "Bingo."

Relief flashed through her. Then shock. Then… horror. She knew what was on her hard drive. She knew what was in her files. "My God," she whispered. "Where did you—"

"Hebert." He flipped it open. "Because you didn't call me…because you didn't trust me…" When the system finished rebooting, he opened her word processing program and pulled up a file. "It's all here in black-and-white."

Her throat burned. Her chest tightened. She looked from the file to Jack.

She'd seen the look before. She'd seen people look at her as if she were a pariah. She'd stood quietly while a bereaved father lashed out at her and his wife cried. She'd caught the way cops looked at her as she scanned grisly photographs, had put up with the insinuations of lawyers who didn't like being on the receiving end of questions.

She'd tolerated reviewers who called her work trash.

At first the bricks hurled at her had hurt; the insults had bruised. But she'd learned to wall herself away from those who did not understand. She'd learned to walk from case to case without being touched. By any of it.

She'd known coming here would be different. She'd known coming here would be worse. There was no shield of anonymity. This wasn't a random case. She couldn't simply walk into and out of all the lives that had been affected. This was her home. These people, the witnesses to that long-ago rainy night, were part of her. She'd known them as long as she could remember. And the victim…

She was the victim.

Her mother was the victim, her brother.

Jack. Jack was the victim, despite how hard he tried to hide behind a cop's strength.

He looked at her now the way the other cops had, with all the scorn and the ridicule. But this time she felt every lash of contempt clear down to her bones. "I don't expect you to understand—"

"Smart girl," he said again, this time quieter. Colder. "I should have put two and two together...but it never even crossed my mind that you could write those books."

Those books. She was accustomed to the insult. Even so, she found her chin coming up. "I write their stories," she corrected. "I write stories for those who can't, for those who suffered. For those who were robbed, cheated." Made victims, taken away too soon. "I make sure they're remembered. I make sure no one forgets what happened to them."

The flatness in his eyes chilled. "I guess the phrase *rest in peace* doesn't mean anything to you then."

The walls pushed in on her, but she didn't let herself move, refused to grant him that power over her, even as the memory shredded.

...may the lord take you into heaven and watch over you, keep you in eternal peace.

"It means everything to me." But she also knew sometimes the words were a flimsy fairy tale, a tidy little bow and ribbon to disguise the truth: there could be no peace, no rest, when the end had been swift and brutal and violent.

When killers walked free.

Swallowing against a throat suddenly raw, she slipped

away from him and crossed to the piano. She wasn't about to let him dissect her as though she were some science project.

It took effort, but she'd learned how to keep it all inside, how to shove the ugliness so deep it couldn't make her shake. Couldn't make her bleed.

"Sweet Mary," he said from behind her. *"Who are you?"*

She didn't want to turn—didn't want to see. Because once she did, once she saw, all those silly fantasies that sometimes sneaked into her sleep, the ones in which nothing stood between her and Jack, would shatter.

"You're gone fourteen years," he said. "Without a word, not even to your mother. And then you waltz back into town like not a day has passed, *to write a book?* About the night your *own father* was murdered?"

He made it sound so ugly.

With the same precision she did everything, she turned. And saw.

He hadn't moved, still stood beside the sofa, his expression condemning her like a criminal in a lineup.

"I'm Camille," she said, and with the words her chest tightened. It had been a long time since she'd allowed herself to use that name. Cameron Monroe was easier, cleaner; it was who she'd become. To be Camille was to go back. To be vulnerable.

And that was something she could never allow.

"All grown-up, but like you said, still me." She still hurt. "I'm still here—and I still remember." Everything. The smiles and the tears and the laughter. The horror. The devastation.

And Jack. She remembered Jack, the way he'd been

before their world blew up in their faces, when he'd looked at her with warmth, rather than suspicion.

"Who am I?" The question, the answer, hurt. But she was done pretending, and she was done hiding. "I'm a woman who remembers what it was like to hear the gunshot that killed my father...to see him collapse." To see him lying there so still. "I remember the voices." The realization that she recognized them. "I remember running." Being chased. The rain. It had come down in vicious sheets. "Hiding."

Jack's eyes went hard and dark, and she knew that he remembered, too. "Damn it, Camille," he said, moving toward her.

She held up a hand before he could reach her. "Don't."

He stopped, let out a rough breath. "That was a long time ago."

"Yes, it was." But time didn't matter, not when lies remained. "But that man is still free." Walking the streets and living his life, hurting those who got in his way— just like so many others who crossed the line between civility and depravity.

"That's what this is about?" he asked. "You go from one crime to the next because you can't stop reliving what happened to your father?"

The stab of disappointment surprised her. She'd known she couldn't walk back into the life she'd left behind. She'd known fractured relationships couldn't be taped back together, that mistakes could not be taken back. Time changed people. She'd told herself that count- less times, had reminded herself that in the years she'd been gone, Jack had fought a war and buried a wife....

But it wasn't until he gave her nothing that she realized how badly she'd wanted to be wrong.

"It's not just my father. What happened that night wasn't only to him. It happened to me. To Gabe." He'd never been the same after that, had grown up virtually overnight. "And to you."

"And you think serving up every dirty detail for public consumption is going to make that better? Make that okay?"

Only in her dreams.

His expression darkened. "Damn it, you have to let it go."

He made it sound so ridiculously simple. Let go. Forget. Move on. Pretend she hadn't seen her father murdered. Pretend she hadn't identified the killer, that everyone hadn't thought she'd made the whole story up.

Pretend she'd never gone to Florida… "I can't."

"Damn it, Camille, he *confessed*," Jack bit out the words. "Lambert told your brother everything."

And then denied it to the judge. She knew that, had heard the details from Saura. With Gabe trapped in a condemned warehouse, Lambert had admitted to killing her father—but he'd also alleged that her father had double-crossed him first. That the shooting had been an accident.

"Everything?" Instinct warned otherwise. She'd seen the look in her father's eyes when she'd found him in her bedroom a few hours before his death. She'd seen the secrets and the determination, the fear. "Are you sure? What if there's more?"

"What are you talking about?"

She gestured toward the laptop. "Someone wants to stop me, Jack. Someone stole my computer and found out about the safe-deposit box, got there before I could." The dots practically connected themselves. "Doesn't that make you wonder why? If the real truth is still out there—"

"Did you ever stop to think, that maybe Marcel Lambert doesn't want you writing this book?"

That went without saying. All his dirty little secrets, that elaborate house of cards he'd built—that she'd let him build by allowing herself not to be heard—was about to go up in flames. "It's not up to him."

The brown of Jack's eyes flashed. "Damn it, this isn't a game. This isn't some benign case that you can whip together and serve to the public. This is *your* life," he said, and then God, he was reaching for her again, crushing the years and mistakes between them to touch her, with all the familiarity of the boy who'd once found her wet and cold and hiding from the man who'd chased her into the swamp. He put his hands to her arms and urged her closer, forcing her up on her toes.

"That man is dangerous," he said, and the rhythm of her heart changed, deepened. "He's killed before."

This, she realized. This was why she had to be careful, why she'd kept her real agenda from him for as long as possible. As a child she'd let Jacques Savoie define her world. If she stood any chance of laying the past to rest, she had to ignore the hot burn in his eyes—and the slow steady thaw in that place she'd meticulously walled off. "I know."

"Then what? You think he's going to sit back and let you write this book? Or do you just not care?"

The questions slammed into her. She cared. More than she'd allowed herself to admit. "I was a kid, Jack, and I was scared. For more than half my life I've lived with the truth about that man…and I'm not going to do it any-more." She stepped back from his arms. "Will he try to stop me?" she asked. "Absolutely. But what kind of woman would I be if I didn't try to stop him first?"

"Alive," he answered point-blank. "You'd be alive."

It shouldn't have been possible to feel a trickle of warmth, even as the chill consumed. "Would I? Are you sure? Because it hasn't felt that way to me."

Not for a long, long time.

"I knew you wouldn't be happy," she said. "I knew you wouldn't want me to write this book…that you'd try to talk me out of it." The way he'd tried to talk her out of everything. Of spreading her wings. Of living.

Of wanting him. "But I never thought…"

"Never thought what?"

It would have been easy to turn away toward the window. To focus on the shadows of the trees shifting against the night sky.

But that was the easy way out, and Camille was done with easy. "When I write a book, I don't do it from the outside looking in." Couldn't. "I go to where it happened. I ask questions." And got door after door slammed in her face. "I go to the police and request files, I pored over every detail, taking pictures and notes, absorbing…."

Absorbing.

"And they just look at me," she said, and absolutely refused to let her voice break again. "The cops, the lawyers. They look at me like I'm the lowest form of low, like I'm scum or a pariah, that I get off wallowing in other people's pain…."

While on the inside, she felt it all, every blow. Every stab. Every gunshot. She felt and she…absorbed.

"And maybe I even understand," she said. "They don't know me. They don't know who I am or what I'm about." That too many nights when she closed her eyes, she could still see her father slumping to the floor. "So it's easy for them to pass judgment. It's easy for them to condemn."

Around them the night shifted in a constant array of shadows, but Jack didn't move—she could barely tell that he breathed.

"But I never thought," she said, careful to keep her voice calm and level, quiet, "you would look at me the same way."

He winced. It was violent and visceral, and it touched her somehow, made her ache in ways she'd never wanted to feel again.

"But I should have," she said. And then she turned, and did what she'd known she would do all along.

She walked away.

She can't move. Everything is still, frozen.

Crouched there in the shadows, she wants to scream. Her brother is home, his best friend. Her mother. They'll come. They'll wake her up. Jack will make it go away....

The words chilled. He looked up from the laptop, didn't want to see. To know. To remember. But he'd already walked away three different times. He'd fed Beauregard and done a quick walk of the grounds, secured the house. He'd flipped on the television, checked in with Russ and Hank.

Poured two fingers of scotch that he wouldn't let himself drink.

Kept going back for more.

There's a door to the backyard. If she can just get
to it—

She, goddamn it. They were Camille's words,
Camille's life. But she used the third person as if she
spoke of someone altogether different....

She does. She yanks it open and runs into the rain.
    Get back here, girl!
    But she keeps running. She can't go back...
can't let the man who killed her father catch her.
He'll kill her, too. She knows that, feels the cold
certainty of that with each step she takes.
    Spanish moss slaps at her; mud slips between
her toes. The lightning keeps flashing, the thunder
shaking the sky. But she never slows. She knows
this land. Jack has shown her. He'll come for her.
That's the thought that drives her. Jack and her
brother. They'll find her—make it all go away.
    Make sure the bad man pays...

Jack shoved from the small table and stood, sent the
chair crashing to the floor as he pivoted and strode for
the spare room, put his hand to the doorknob.
    And turned.
    She lay there, goddamn it. She lay on her side, in his
spare bed. Sleeping.
    Quietly—nice and freaking slow—he closed the door
and walked away.

There were no prints at his grandmother's, or
Camille's childhood home. The only tire tracks belonged

to Saura's convertible and Jack's squad car. There was nothing out of place, nothing broken, nothing to indicate anyone other than Jack and Camille had been at the house the night before. If he hadn't been there himself, Jack would have thought—

She's delusional...he'd heard the principal of their high school say. *Makes up things....*

A wild child, the woman in the trailer next door had said.

Why, if I didn't know better, the sheriff had once remarked, *I'd think she has a—*

Death wish.

Jack shoved aside his fourth cup of coffee. She couldn't go anywhere, he knew that. Unless she went on foot. Russ was stationed at the end of the drive. Beauregard was out front. But—

Death wish.

The words, the memory of the chilling passages he'd read the night before, pushed him to the front door. He kept trying to think of her as she'd once been, Gabe's little sister, freckles and pigtails and all. But the truth was she hadn't been that girl since the night she'd seen her father die. She'd changed after that, started taking chances, daring her family to stop her. They'd caught her drinking, experimenting—

Kiss me, Jack...teach me how.

He'd smelled the beer on her breath, but he'd also seen the stabbing desperation in her eyes. That's why he'd never told Gabe. That's why he'd tried to help her himself...even as he'd wanted to turn her over his knee or lock her away. The writing had been on the wall. She was on a collision course with trouble.

Yanking at the screen door, he strode onto the porch.

No matter how many years had passed, little had changed. It wasn't the senselessness of her father's death that drove her, but the fact that no one took her seriously. No one believed her. No one had stood by—

Beauregard came bounding from the tree line—

Alone.

Chapter 9

For a cruel second, everything stopped. Jack's heart slammed hard. He started to run as the moment slipped back into focus and he saw the bright yellow Frisbee in his dog's mouth…and heard Camille laugh.

"Good boy!" she praised as the dog raced up and dropped the toy, panting. Camille hugged him, then launched the Frisbee toward the pines.

With an excited bark, Beauregard took off.

In the middle of an overgrown flower bed, Camille knelt with gloves on her hands and a stack of weeds by her knees. With the early-morning sun raining down on her, she picked up the rusted pruning sheers and went to work on an out-of-control rosebush.

Roses, Jack…please. We have to have roses….

The memory stopped him. He stared at Camille excavating the rosebushes his wife had insisted on planting. She'd tended them daily….

That should have been his first clue. When the roses had stopped blooming, when they'd started growing tall and spindly. When the black spots had overtaken the lush green. He should have known, should have realized that Susan had stopped caring.

He saw now the glow on Camille's face as she again greeted Beauregard and launched the yellow disc. Again went to work on restoring the roses.

The wind blew, he knew that. He could see the Spanish moss swaying. For the first time in over a year, the warmth rushed up against his face.

He felt only cold.

Quietly, he stepped from the porch and went back inside. Shut the door.

She knew the second he left. She knelt with her shirt caught on a thorn and tried to breathe, told herself not to turn. Not to look. But she glanced over her shoulder anyway, and found the porch deserted. The way she'd known it would be.

Frowning, she looked up as Beauregard dashed back with the Frisbee. "Such a good boy," she told him, taking the well-chewed toy and tossing it toward the trees.

The temptation to follow was strong. She could lose herself in the woods, work her way back to the highway. There she could hitch a ride to her rental. Jack would notice her gone, and he would follow. But she'd not said a word about the pictures she'd taken of the map. She could start looking without him.

She stood and pulled off the gloves. She could. She

could slip into the woods. She could follow her father's map. No one would know.

Beauregard barked excitedly and came galloping back.

"Come on, boy," she said, turning to the house. Because it was the smart thing to do, she told herself. Jack was a cop. Lambert was getting desperate. If by some chance he followed, tried to stop her—

That's why she went back into the house. She knew what happened when people took unnecessary risks— she'd written about the outcomes too many times: the serial rapist who coerced women into opening their doors by claiming to be looking for a lost puppy named Sam. And the woman in San Jose, the one who'd agreed to help a crippled man into his van. She'd been brutally assaulted, used as a sex toy for five days until her body had given out.

That's why Camille gave Beauregard a smooch, then walked into the stillness. Because it was the smart thing to do. The safe thing.

Not because she couldn't stop thinking about the gleam in Jack's eyes when he'd stood in the shadows of his living room.

We'd be in my bed...naked.

The quiet drew her to the kitchen, where she found him at the sink. In his left hand he held an old mug with a hand-painted crawfish on it. His right hand was in a fist. His athletic shorts were gray and baggy, his tank top white.

Even standing that way, all alone and isolated, he made her blood hum.

"It was hers, wasn't it?" she asked.

He stiffened.

"The rose garden." The one neglected to the point of abuse. "It was your wife's."

He put the mug on the counter, but did not turn. His shoulders, so much wider and wearier than all those years ago, rose with his breath. "Yes."

The weeds had been everywhere, their roots deep and tangled. The bushes themselves had been spindly, the leaves covered by black spots and aphids, the stalks depleted by dead wood.

"Is that why it bothered you to see me out there?" The question was quiet, even though there was nothing quiet inside her. If not for what Saura had told her, Camille would have had no idea about Jack's wife. There was no trace of her—not in the house in which she'd once lived, the garden she'd once tended. The man who'd once pledged to love her forever.

The reality of that scraped. Not that Jack had asked another woman to be his wife, but that he could erase her from his life so completely. "Because I was trespassing on hallowed ground?"

A strangled sound broke from his throat. He twisted toward her, came close to stopping her breath with the shadows in his eyes and the nasty scar on his right thigh. "It's not hallowed ground."

"Then why?" Questions surged. Why wouldn't Jack talk about his wife? Why had he abandoned her garden, something that had clearly once meant a lot to her—the trio of weathered angel statues told Camille that. And the poem on a rock.

And most troubling of all, why didn't she see even a trace of pain in his eyes. "Why didn't you say anything?"

The slight twist to his mouth was the only warning she got. "Just what is it you want me to say, sugar?" Not *'tite chat.* "You want me to bring you some ice-cold lemonade and talk about plans for your book? Just how much detail you plan to—"

Frustration nudged in. "Jack—"

His smile was slow, tortured. "Or maybe you'd rather not talk at all…."

Before the tactic had worked. She'd gotten too close, and he'd chosen to push her away by making it clear what he wanted to do with her—if she'd been a stranger.

But she wasn't a stranger—and she was done being manipulated.

"Now that's a real darn good idea," she said, stepping toward him—and had to wonder if he realized he was the one who'd taken a step back.

With a quick glance around the utilitarian kitchen, she gestured toward one of the rail-back chairs at the table. "Sit."

The planes of his face, so wide and classically Cajun, tightened. "Now why would I want to do that?"

"Because I asked you to."

"Then what?" The clipped words were hard. The gleam in his eye was not. "You gonna tie me up?"

"Do I need to?"

His gaze met hers, and for a dizzying moment all those walls between them, those tacked together of regret and guilt, the sins of a long-ago storm and the threats still lurking in the shadows, fell away. There was only a man and a woman, and the slow burn of awareness: the rules had changed. The dynamics had shifted. They weren't children anymore.

And the games they played had irrevocable consequences.

"Fair is fair," he drawled with a wicked little smile, then blew her mind by doing as she asked. He lowered his big body into the small chair. It was almost as if he wanted—

Almost as if he wanted to find out what came next as badly as she did.

She stepped toward him. "Now turn around."

His tank top fell loosely against his shoulders. "Why's that?" he asked. "You gonna do something you don't want me to see?" The brown of his eyes deepened. Darkened. "Or maybe…there's something *you* don't want to see?"

Her heart kicked. She knew what he was doing, playing the game he'd started the night before. Chicken, they'd called it as children. Get on a collision course and start walking, running, see who would blink first. Who would turn away.

Who would run.

"Maybe I want you to let go." To see if he could. From her earliest memories he'd always needed to be in control. That was nothing new. But there was a jagged edge to the need now, a broken desperation that had not been there before. It was almost as if—

It wasn't *almost as if.* It *was.* All along the interstate stood trees, big, tall, most of them bent. Only a few stood as they had before, unmoved despite the carnage around them. They'd endured and they'd survived, while so many around them had fallen.

"But you can't do that, can you? You can't let go, not even for a second…not even to enjoy."

The change was subtle. His eyes darkened, went languorous and sleepy. "A man doesn't have to let go to enjoy, *cher*."

Cher. The lazy, smoky endearment did vicious things to the point she was trying to make.

"You might be surprised." Then, while he sat there in that small chair, his big body twisted toward hers, she lifted her hands to his shoulders.

"You're tense." Hot. She worked her fingers against the corded muscles of his neck and his back, the way she'd done so many times before. Then there had been the excitement, the giddiness of a girl with dreams.

Now the burn streaked to her bone.

Once this man had been a dreamer. Once, Jacques Savoie, the skinny kid with the hand-me-down clothes and worn-out tennis shoes, had talked of the future. He was going to join the Air Force. He was going to serve his country. He'd smiled and he'd laughed, even when Camille had found him standing outside her kitchen, listening to her mother and father arguing about Jack's father. *He's no good,* her mother always said. *Cares more about that ridiculous stained glass window than his own kid....*

A dreamer, Camille's father had corrected. Gator Savoie was a man who believed in pursuing his dreams, his passion.... He didn't believe in boundaries, in quitting. He didn't believe in limits.

But then Camille's father died, and Gator walked out of a bar and into the fog. Some thought he was dead, by his own hand or someone else's. Others thought he was running. Hiding. A coward.

At the time, Jack had been fifteen, grown-up enough to step forward when his mother's world crumbled. He never complained, just stepped in to steady the ship.

He'd worked at the grocery and mowed lawns, did odd jobs around town; he'd cared for his mother after she found a lump in her breast. But all the while, he'd never stopped dreaming about flying F-16s. Never stopped believing it would happen.

And he never, not once, stopped caring.

Not for his mother—not for Camille. Even when she'd pushed him. Even when she'd lashed out. Even when she'd tried to tempt him, hoping she could make him see her as something other than his best friend's little sister. She'd offered him back rubs, had run her hands along his spine, just as she did now. The more responsibility he heaped onto his shoulders, the more desperate she'd become to... She didn't know what.

It was only that one night that she'd gone too far.

From outside the kitchen window the air-conditioning kicked on, and against her arms Camille felt the rush of air. But the heat, the stillness, deepened.

Jacques Savoie had gone after his dreams, but he'd come home without them.

And deep inside, even though she'd promised herself she would never let herself be vulnerable to this man again, that she would walk into town, then walk right back out, Camille wanted to know why.

"You have to let go." The words were quiet, gentle. The pressure of her fingertips was not. "Jacques...you have to let go."

To quit treating her as if she were the enemy.

"Breathe," she murmured, using her thumbs to release a knot beneath his left shoulder blade. "Quit trying to carry everything on your shoulders."

The rough sound was the only warning she got. He

closed his eyes and dropped his head, almost seemed to sag beneath the weight he did not want anyone else to see. Quietly she accepted the little surrender and kept on working, squeezing and rubbing against his back. There were scars, she noted. Scars she could feel with her fingers, and those she felt with her heart.

Both on the outside, and the inside.

"Everything's going to be okay," she told him, but as soon as the words left her mouth, the bitter aftertaste of a lie set in.

Everything was not going to be okay. She would write her book. She would do whatever it took to make sure Marcel Lambert went down. And then, for the first time in two decades, she would be free. Doors would finally close, the final chapter would be written. She'd be able to move on, move forward.

But Jack…

She closed her eyes and slid her hands along the warmth of his flesh, felt her throat tighten. Hard cords of tension riddled his back. She worked against them, tried to make them loosen. *Let go…*

"Lower."

The muttered word drifted through her as if somehow he'd turned the tables while she closed her eyes, and now he was the one who touched. In places she didn't want to be touched. She opened her eyes and swallowed hard, slid her hands toward his lower back. "Here?"

"Lower." It was more a rasp than a word, stilling her hands.

"Jack—"

"Not yet," he murmured. "You're not quite there yet, darlin'."

Heat licked deep, unleashing the little voice inside, the one that shouted for her to step back. "Where?" Her throat burned on the question. She looked at him seated in the rail-back chair, his head bowed forward. "Where do you want me?"

He twisted toward her, all but eviscerated her with the slow burn in his eyes. "This isn't about what I want, sugar. This is all about you."

Everything inside of her stilled.

"You want in, right?" Sunlight glinted through the window, but shadows fell against the bruise of his temple. "You want inside. You want to know where it hurts. Isn't that what this is all about?"

She knew where it hurt. "You make it sound like a crime."

"What then?" he asked in that same husky, lazy bedroom voice. "You find the weak spot, and then what? You going to fix me? Make everything okay?"

Her throat tightened. "It's not weakness—"

Nothing prepared her for his laugh. It rumbled from his throat, and came horribly close to shattering her heart. "Tell me something, sugar. Has this worked in the past?"

This time she did retreat. And this time she did let go.

"Is this how you do all that research you're acclaimed for?" he asked. "This how you find out all those dirty little secrets no one wants you to know?"

She told herself the insinuation didn't hurt. *"What?"*

He moved so fast she had no time to prepare, no time to twist away before his hand snagged hers. "You come in here and put your hands all over me," he said with a slow squeeze, "look at me with those goddamn lost eyes…."

Shock dulled her to the pain. "Jack, no—"

"What am I supposed to do now?" The question was ragged almost, but with it he stood and tugged her closer. "What is it you want? This?" His mouth was against hers. His lips warm, soft. Moving.

Damning.

He pulled back enough for their eyes to meet. "Then what? We go to bed? Find out what would happen if we really were strangers?"

She tried to escape, but somehow he'd backed her against the counter. He held her there, kept her hands in his. "Is that how it works? You want me so blinded by what you do to me that I can't think straight?"

Twist away, that was the smart thing to do. But something in Jack's voice, the broken edge, the pain—*the desperation*—pulsed through her.

"That suddenly the rules become yours…." In that moment, with his body to hers, she knew that he was finally seeing her, the woman she'd become, not the girl she'd been. "That I forget that someone went after you last night—that someone wants to *hurt* you?"

She swallowed, tried to breathe. Think.

"Forget about your book." He went on in that same dark magic voice, the one that made everything blur, shift. "That someone wants to stop you? Is that what you want?"

"No." It was barely a whisper.

"Then *what?*" The question sounded torn from him. "What the hell is it you want me to do?"

The answer sliced deep. She wanted him to quit pushing her away. To quit shutting himself off. To quit holding on so tight.

She wanted him to let go—and she wanted to be the one to show him that he would not fall.

"What if I said yes?" She grabbed the gauntlet he'd thrown down and tossed it back at him. "What if I said I do want to be strangers…to see what would happen?"

His eyes darkened. "So that's what this is about. Why you didn't lock your door last night? Because you want to pretend you're not the girl who gets off on shoving hot pokers at me? That folks don't say it was my daddy who killed your daddy? That he didn't work for Marcel Lambert? That he wasn't just a plant—a spy?"

"No—"

"You want to pretend we didn't get drunk, that everything didn't spin out of control—"

"No," she whispered, but even as she said the word, she had to wonder. "That's not what this is about." It would be easier that way, she knew, if they could erase all those messy ties that bound them together. "I just want you to see me—"

"I see you," he drawled with a glitter to his eyes. "But you also need to trust that I know what I'm doing here. I know who I am, who you are." He lifted a hand to her face, let it fall without touching. "Men like me…we don't make love to women like you. We—"

"Men like you?" It was her turn to stop him. "Just what kind of man do you want me to think you are?"

He released her so fast she sagged against the counter. "Russ is around back," he said, crossing the brightly lit kitchen. At the back door, he jabbed his finger against four keys on the security pad. "If you even think about doing something foolish—"

She squared her shoulders, even as the ache wound deep. "You'll know."

Then he was gone, pushing open the door and

striding into the early afternoon, leaving her acutely
aware of the line she'd tried to cross—and the question
he'd refused to answer.

What kind of man do you want me to think you are?

Jack ran.

Around him the land of his childhood closed in, trees
that had stood for generations lying like forgotten pick-
up-sticks, while cypress knees and aboveground roots
created a maze of land mines. Still he ran, and still he
tested himself, closing his eyes, relying on instinct to
keep him from falling on his face.

It was the same instinct he'd ignored that hot day outside
of Kirkuk when he'd seen a group of small children and
approached them with water and chocolate bars.

Two steps ahead Beauregard raced along. Jack could
hear him breathing, could hear the dog's paws come
down on the decaying leaves. "Datta, boy," he praised,
slipping into the dialect of his youth. And with the words
he kicked it up a notch.

He'd missed this. While in the Middle East, surrounded by desert and sky, he'd missed the lush land of
his birth. He'd missed the trees and the green, the water.
He'd sometimes wandered out at night while the wind
howled and the sand lashed his face—

Throwing his head back, he looked up through the
dense, shifting canopy of leaves, and felt everything
inside of him tighten.

She didn't belong here, damn it. Time had moved
forward. She was part of the past, a reminder of a lifetime
that had died long ago.

As a kid, he'd learned everything had a place. Shoes

went under the bed, dirty clothes in the hamper, albums on the shelf. Schoolbooks went on the desk his grandfather had made for him. If he left anything out of place…

I don't have time for this, boy! How many times do I have to tell you to keep your things away from my work?

Jack stumbled against a protruding root and staggered forward. Everything had a place. Gabe was his friend. Camille was his wild child sister.…

He ignored the protest of his thigh and ran harder, pushing off with his left foot to hurdle a fallen pine.

Nothing fit in a tidy place anymore. Everything he'd ever worked toward, everything he'd ever wanted…

Had blown up in his face.

And Camille…she didn't belong here, damn it. She belonged to his past, the same as his father and Susan, his career. Camille didn't belong here, now, with her lies and her secrets, her hidden agendas, tearing through his life like the hurricane that was her namesake. He didn't want to look at her and see those goddamn freckles, to remember.

To want.

To realize how far he would go to make sure…

He crushed the thought, demolished it, knew too damn good and well what happened when a man let go, and need took over.

I just want you to see me.

He did. He saw her.

That was the problem.

By all accounts, Gator Savoie was a drifter. The town drunk. No one knows where he came from—

or where he went. If he committed murder, if he stole—or if he crossed the wrong man.

His friendship with Troy Fontenot was as unlikely as a hurricane in May. Troy was a learned man, a history professor. He loved his wife and children, didn't drink, didn't smoke. He only had one vice…one obsession.

Gator had many. A high school dropout, he liked his whiskey and his Marlboro cigarettes, his women—even after he married and became a father. Of course, some say the child came first….

Camille frowned—Jack may have been conceived before his parents married, but he'd never come first.

They made an odd pair, but Troy was always collecting strays, and Gator was no different. Soon Gator was as knee-deep in Troy's obsession as if he'd been breathing it his whole life….

Thirty minutes had passed since Jack and Beauregard took off for the woods. They'd been running… The temptation to go to the porch was strong, but she kept writing.

Some say Gator was on Lambert's payroll. That his job was to befriend Troy, keep an eye on him. That he was the one in the study that night, that he was the one who'd killed his so-called friend, chased the man's daughter into the swamp….

That was the angle Camille's editor wanted to play—

friend versus friend. Scandal. Betrayal. But Camille had refused. Friend versus friend was not the story of her father's death. Greed was. Deception.

He walked into a bar the night after Troy died. When he walked out, he was never seen again. His truck remained in the parking lot. His closet was full, his bank account untouched. Either Gator Savoie was running—or he was dead.

Chances are—

The sound of the door slamming broke the thought. Camille looked up as heavy footsteps sounded, found Jack emerging from the kitchen. Sunlight glistened off the sheen on his flesh—his tank top and shorts were damp. In his hand he held a glass of water. And in his eyes she saw…

Nothing. Not familiarity. Not warmth. Not the slow gleam of seduction. Just the blank look of a man who knew how to wash it all white.

He'd been gone over an hour. His shoes were dirty. There was a trickle of blood along his forearm. His hand was at his thigh.

Camille flicked her gaze back to her notes while Jack crossed the room behind her. His footsteps told her he walked down the hall. The sound of a door closing told her he did not want her to follow.

The sound of water running through the pipes told her he was in the shower.

She blinked and tried to focus, but the image taunted her. Of Jack. Standing in the old porcelain bathtub, with his head bent under the spray. His eyes would be closed.

Water would sluice down his shoulders and his stomach, his hips, his legs....

Shoving the image aside, Camille glanced out the window, where Beauregard danced beneath an old pecan tree. She watched for a few seconds before reaching for the pictures she'd taken the day before. Her father's map. She'd studied the photos deep into the night, long after she'd closed the door to Jack. And with the light of dawn, as she'd let herself start to free-write, the memory had come. Of the trip she'd taken with her father two weeks before his death—to a barrier island.

Isle Dernier, it was called. Last Island. And Camille would bet her life that there'd been far more to the excursion than her father had let on.

She heard the screech first, a distorted noise from the bathroom as if Jack had ripped open the shower curtain.

The thud shattered that illusion.

Chapter 10

Everything inside Camille stopped. She dropped the picture and stood, turned toward the hallway. "Jack?"

From behind the closed door the water ran—but Jack did not respond.

The slow crawl of dread made no sense. Her voice was soft. He hadn't heard. That was all.

But she made her way toward the door anyway, leaving behind the wash of sunlight and stepping into the shadows. "Jack?"

Her heart slammed. And something cold and dark lodged in her throat. She told herself not to run, that she was being ridiculous. But her feet started moving—and she ran. "Jack!"

The closed door loomed. "Answer me!" she shouted, lunging for the little glass knob.

She sensed the movement too late. She tried to twist,

but he was already there, closing in on her and yanking her against his chest. "Don't try anything stupid, sweet girl, and no one gets hurt."

Sweet girl. The words, the voice, stabbed. She stiffened against the tall man's grip, tried to think. "Jack—"

"Took something that doesn't belong to him," the man said. "And now you're going to give it back."

The water pounded from inside the small bathroom, steady. Constant. "What did you do to him? You have to let me—"

"I don't have to let you do anything," he said in that same awful raspy voice, the one that had haunted her nightmares for too many years. And to prove his words, he shifted a hand against her back, and she felt the gun. "But *you* do."

Inside she started to shake. "I don't know what you're talking about."

"Of course you do," Marcel Lambert said. "I'm talking about your daddy's map…the one you came home to find."

Her breath caught. Lambert claimed the stained glass had been destroyed the night her father died. That Troy Fontenot had planned to double-cross him, sell him out.

If that were true, there was no need for the map.

Excitement tangled with dread. She'd been right all along. Her father *had* been trying to tell her something.

"I don't have it," she snapped at Lambert. "Jack does—it's at the station."

"No," he said slowly. "It's not."

"Jack—"

"Brought the file home with him."

Jack hadn't said a word. And now he lay on the other side of the closed door, in the shower. The water was running.

"What did you do to him?" she demanded again, and this time she twisted.

The memory almost sent her to her knees.

Those eyes… Dark and magnetic, they gleamed at her from two small holes in the ski mask. And his mouth—she remembered that mouth, the way it had moved as if in slow motion. Calling her name—ordering her to stop.

But she hadn't stopped. She'd run, and she'd run, out into the night, the storm, as fast as she could.

"The map," he said now, standing there so tall and un-yielding, a coward to the bone. "And then we'll worry about Jacques."

She looked down at the 9mm in his gloved hand, then up at his dead flat eyes. "You won't use that."

"Is that a chance you want to take?"

"It's not me taking chances. You're the one awaiting trial. I'm a public figure. It's no secret I'm here research-ing a book. If I turn up dead—"

This time the laugh was darkly pleased. "That's where you're wrong, sweet girl. I'm not awaiting trial."

The words slammed into her. But she pushed them aside, knew they were a lie. There were no more players in this game. Everyone else was already dead.

Dead…

She wrenched from Lambert and lunged for the door, grabbed the knob and turned. He caught her as the door flung open. "Damn it, girl—"

Everything flashed, turned white except for the sight of the man sprawled naked in the bathtub, the flimsy plastic curtain pulled down around him. "Jack!"

Lambert yanked her back before she could take a

second step. "There's only one way you can help him!" he snarled, dragging her from the bathroom.

She fought him, rammed her elbow into his gut and stomped her foot down on his, went for his forearm with her teeth. "You bastard! I'm—"

"Going to help Jacques, yes, I know." His voice was cold, bland. "Just give me what I want, and then you can have what you want."

She stilled, sucked in a sharp breath.

"You can't stop me, sweet girl. No one can. Not Jacques or the deputy posted at the end of the drive, not that lazy old dog—"

Beauregard. Earlier he'd been barking, agitated. Now there was only silence. "No…"

Lambert held her tighter. "Pretty quiet, isn't it?"

Horror surged. Denial pierced. But with it came a twist of reality: this man had killed before.

"Now be a good girl and find me that map."

Twenty years of grief and injustice closed in on her. She turned slowly, felt the gun jab into her back. Lambert matched her step for step. The truth skirted close behind. For too long she'd been running, letting this man dictate her every move. Her life. That he would come to her here, now, this way.

He would not win.

At the closed door across the hall she put her hand to the knob and pushed inside, instinctively stopped.

The big bed dominated the spacious room. A simple black comforter covered the king mattress, three pillows lined up along the top. There was nothing else, no throw pillows, no sign a woman had ever shared this room. The furniture was big and dark, simple. There was nothing on top of the chest of drawers, no pictures or pocket change or wallet, not a watch or a ring, his gun—*nothing*.

The small chest beside his bed wasn't much different. A brass lamp sat in the center, with a digital clock beside the bed—and a book propped open on top. Secret Sins.

"What are you waiting for, Cami-girl?"

Inside, everything tightened. Disgust rushed in. Knowing what had to be done, she moved toward the bed and went down on her knees in front of the nightstand. She didn't touch the book, though, didn't check to see what chapter he'd been reading. She knew what was in the book. She knew the horrors she'd written about. She knew the pain. The tragedy.

With hands she refused to let shake, she pulled open the top drawer and found a stack of paperbacks. Not fiction, though. Nonfiction, books about seizing the moment and the meaning of life, books with big questions and few answers. There was a pad of paper and a pen—but nothing else. No map, and no gun.

The bottom drawer contained much the same.

"Under the bed," Lambert instructed.

She did as he said, went down to look under the mattress—but saw only an old pair of athletic shoes and a well-chewed dog toy.

Between the mattresses failed to yield anything, either.

With the gun jabbed between her ribs, she stood and moved toward the dresser, resisted the temptation to spin. And fight. Maybe she could take him. Maybe she couldn't. She knew self-defense. She'd been trained. She knew—

Jack sprawled, unconscious, naked in the bathtub.

The top drawer held socks. The next drawer held... boxers. It was an odd time to smile, but her mouth curved.

Big tough Jacques Savoie was a boxer man. She put her hands to the soft cotton and ignored the sensation, focused on looking for the map.

The third drawer held T-shirts; the fourth held shorts. The fifth...

She went down on her knees and reached for the photograph. Slowly she lifted it. In the shadows of Jack's bedroom, Camille looked down at the photo she'd found in the bottom drawer of his dresser, a photo discolored by time, the image faded. But the smiles touched her anyway.

"Jack," she whispered without voice, running her finger first along his image, then Gabe's, then her own.

"Hurry it up," Lambert commanded, but Camille couldn't move. Could only touch the long-ago image of her and Jack and Gabe just returned from a crawfishing expedition, their clothes dirty, her braids tattered, their smiles forever frozen.

Much as he was now frozen inside.

But he'd kept the picture tucked safely in the bottom of his dresser....

With an ache in her chest, she returned the photo and shut the drawer, turned back toward the bed. It was instinct that had her returning to the nightstand and reaching for the book he'd left open. Instinct that had her flipping through the pages—and finding the folded paper stashed in the back.

"Open it," Lambert instructed, but she was already unfolding the edges. "Sweet Mary." He inhaled when her father's handwriting came into view, the intricately drawn map Troy and Gator had created decades before.

The same map she'd photographed alongside the road.

"Finally…" Lambert snatched the map and jabbed the gun against her back. "Get up."

"You said—"

"The closet. Now."

Dark possibilities hammered through her. *Jack…* "You have what you want. Now just go—"

"And let you come after me? I don't think so," he snarled with another jab of the gun. He took her by the arm and shoved her toward the closet. "Get inside."

Her throat tightened. She wanted to spin and fight, to drive a knee into his groin and take him down. But Jack lay unconscious….

Biting down on her lip, she walked into the closet and allowed Lambert to take her arms and pull them behind her back, bind her wrists together.

She let the grim images razor through her. She'd been young then, scared and hurt, easily manipulated. But she was a woman now, and the rules were her own.

Through the vertigo of memory she felt him step back, heard the door close. Then darkness. She listened while he dragged a chair across the floor, heard him shove it against the door handle. Then…nothing.

Seconds dragged into minutes. She listened, waited. Lambert thought he was in control. He thought she was the child she'd been all those years ago, when he'd tracked her to Florida.

Lambert was wrong.

She counted to fifty, waited until she heard the echo of the door closing. Then she spun and rammed her shoulder against the door. "Jack!"

Determination drove her. With her hands behind her back she reached for the knob and turned it, ignored the throb of pain while shoving with her shoulder. Over, and over. "Jack!"

Russ waited at the end of the drive. Lambert would have come through the woods. If she could get to the phone—

The door gave way and she spilled into the bedroom, went down hard against the bare floor. The impact of bone against wood jolted, but she scrambled to her feet and ran for the bathroom.

The door still hung open. The water still ran. And Jack…Jack still lay beneath the white shower curtain.

"Jack!" she shouted, and then, twisting her hands against the bindings, she ran.

His name echoed through the storm, soft, agitated. He spun toward it, looked for her. But everywhere he turned, shadows stretched and spilled, darkened. And the rain kept falling. Not warm anymore. But cold. Relentless.

"God," she whispered. "Please."

The violence of the storm lashed at him, pulled, but he strained against it and fought, worked to crack open an eye. If he could see her—

The rain stopped.

"Hang on," she murmured. "Just hang on and I'll get help."

Cold air rushed his body. He recoiled against it, twisted—and felt her. The warmth washed through him, soft and silken, draped over him. He forced open his eyes and blinked, brought her into focus. With blond hair scraggling against her face, she leaned over him, stared through eyes damp and worried. "Jack?"

The shadows shifted, turned into a gossamer fog. He blinked, tried to bring her into focus. "Cami?"

"You're okay," she whispered, and God help him, he would have sworn her voice broke on the words. Cami's voice, the one that had been so tough and strong and defiant. "Everything's going to be okay. Just—"

He reached for her, took her by the arms—realized she was as wet as he was. And fully clothed. *Straddling him.* With a hard slam of adrenaline he twisted and saw the tub, felt the porcelain beneath his back.

"What the hell—" he started to say, but then she was leaning closer, pressing the softness of her body to his.

"Easy," she said. "You're hurt—"

He jerked beneath her and tried to sit but only succeeded in bringing her fully onto his lap. It all started to come back to him, the wooziness and the disorientation. The shower had started to spin. He'd reached for the curtain, had just wanted to close his eyes....

"Son of a bitch!" He reached for her and put his hands to her body, urged her close. "I have to get you out of here before—"

The wince stopped him. He pulled back, realized he was too late. "Sweet God." She was leaning over him, trying to warm him, but she hadn't touched him. Not with her hands. Her arms were behind her back at an unnatural angle....

Swearing softly, he slid his hands against her damp shirt and found the gaudy tie his secretary had given him for Christmas wrapped around Camille's wrists. "Goddamn it."

He'd been drugged. He'd gone down like a freaking baby, left Camille alone and vulnerable.

He brought his hands to her wrists and worked at the insidious knot, acutely aware of the thready rhythm of her heart pulsing against his chest. "He got to you. He—"

"No, Jack. I'm fine. I—"

He pulled back and brought his hands to her face. "Tell me," he said, shoving all those hard, broken edges down deep, refusing to let them puncture his voice. "Tell me what he did to you."

Because someone was so freaking going to pay.

But Camille kept looking at him through those wide, amazing eyes—the same way she'd looked at him when he'd found her after she'd witnessed her father's death. She'd been wet then, too. Shaking. But she wasn't shaking now. She was...completely calm.

"Nothing," she said. "He didn't do anything to me. It wasn't me he wanted."

Everything slowed, clicked viciously. She was wet, but fully clothed. She wasn't hurt. There was no blood. He was the one who'd been incapacitated. Which meant— "The map."

Her eyes darkened, and he had his answer.

He didn't want to let go, didn't want to stop touching. But he couldn't let her kneel there in the shower with her hands tied behind her back. "Son of a bitch," he hissed, and the words were quiet, but lethal.

Forcing himself to let go, he untangled himself from the plastic shower curtain and lunged from the tub, refused to let his stiff right leg buckle. From the medicine cabinet he retrieved the small scissors, then turned back and went down on his knees. The silk bindings fell away leaving deep red gouges in her wrists. "He's a dead man."

She twisted toward him, damn near slayed him with the ferocity in her eyes.

"You were right," he said, reaching for her hand to help her from the tub. She stepped over the side and into his arms, looked up with a trust that almost sent him right back to his knees. "About everything," he said. "That man thinks he's above the law. It's just a game to him. He thinks he can play people like they're pawns—"

Something broken flashed through her eyes.

"Cami?"

But then the shine of courage was back, the same tenaciousness he'd seen too damn many times in Iraq. And it was all he could do to keep from driving his fist into the wall. He'd set the trap, laid out the bait. But he'd never imagined it would be Camille who faced the fire while Jack lay incapacitated in his own bathtub.

"There's more…"

The soft words punched, had him looking down into her upturned face. "You said he didn't hurt—"

"Not me," she said, and now it was she who touched, she who lifted a hand to his face. "Beauregard."

Spanish moss slapped them. Jack zigzagged around a series of tree stumps, hurdled over two fallen pines. He ran fast and hard, with only a slight limp, not pausing to assess or navigate, as if he knew every twist and turn, every tree, every obstacle by heart.

"Beauregard!"

The edge to his voice tightened the vise around Camille's heart.

"Réponds mon chien!" Answer me! *"Où vous êtes?"* Where are you?

Camille raced behind him, tried to keep pace. But she didn't ask him to slow, didn't *want* him to slow. No matter how long she lived, she'd never forget the drain of color from Jack's face when she'd repeated Lambert's taunts and insinuations.

For a moment he'd stood there, holding her, and she'd known he was torn, still worried about her, not wanting to leave her but needing to find Beauregard. *Let's go,* she'd told him, and that was all the encouragement he needed. He didn't waste time grabbing a towel, just ripped from her and ran into his bedroom, pulled on a pair of underwear and gym shorts, shoved his feet into his old athletic shoes, then ran for the back door.

From the hall closet, he grabbed his service revolver.

In the kitchen, Camille retrieved her mobile phone. She tossed it to him as they passed the rose bed, ran along behind him as he called Russ and Detective D'Ambrosia, barked out orders and demanded a locale on Marcel Lambert.

I'm not awaiting trial.

The words chased Camille through the woods. Typical summer in Louisiana, clouds had rolled in, thickened. The sky was heavy now. In the distance, thunder rumbled.

"Bo-Bo!" Jack called. "Answer Papa!"

Papa. She tripped on the word, staggered against a tangle of vines. *Papa.* Jack had lost his father and his wife, his dream of flying fighter planes. But Beauregard...

Pretty quiet, isn't it?

"Come on, boy!" This time it was Camille who called for him, Camille whose voice broke. "Beauregard!"

Jack twisted toward her, revealing the most scorched earth eyes she'd ever seen.

"Go!" she told him. "I'm fine."

But he slowed, held out his hand. "There's a creek ahead—"

"I know." She remembered. She knew this land, not as well as he did, but she'd grown up here, too. She'd traipsed the woods…usually a few steps behind Jack and her brother.

But he was holding out a hand to her now, and she went to him, took his hand and ignored the stitch in her side.

"Did he say anything else?" Jack asked. "Did he give any indication—"

"No," she told him. "I heard Beau barking a few minutes before you fell. He was agitated. I thought it was a squirrel." But it hadn't been. It had been Marcel Lambert.

Or had it?

The nasty thought niggled at her. Marcel Lambert would be ridiculously bold to come after her in broad daylight. He could have hired someone, that was true. But those eyes…

"Beauregard!"

They heard it simultaneously, more of a whimper than a bark. *"Mon Dieu,"* Jack breathed, and ran faster, harder. She let him go, let him charge into the muddy waters of the creek toward the other side, where something yellow lay slumped against the base of an oak.

Her heart surged. She followed, waded into the thigh-high water and found Jack on the other side, reaching for his dog.

"Is he—" A pair of bottomless chocolate eyes gazed up at her and blinked, sent her to her knees. "Beau…"

The big muscular dog lifted his face toward her hand, nuzzled her palm, then whimpered again.

"He tied him up." Jack bit out the words. He reached into his pocket and pulled out a small utility knife, flicked it open and used the blade to sever the rope looped around Beauregard's collar. "There now," he said, and his voice was soft, soothing. "Papa's here."

Camille rocked back and watched, tried to breathe. Somewhere along the line rain had started to fall—she hadn't even noticed. "Thank God," she whispered.

With his dog in his lap, Jack looked up, and everything else fell away. His eyes, so isolated and...charged, met hers. And for a moment he looked at her while the rain came down and the sky rumbled, while lightning streaked. And then he was curving a hand around her rib cage and pulling her closer, bracketing his other hand behind her head.

No words were spoken. No words were necessary. Maybe his mouth found hers first. Or maybe it was she who pushed up and into him. Or maybe they both reached, and they both found. She didn't know, didn't care, only knew that she needed his mouth on hers. She closed her eyes and let the sensation wash through her, knew she could drown in the feel of his lips, the lingering taste of peppermint and desire, of brutality.

"Mon chou..." He kissed her deeper. She opened to him, thrilled to the warmth of his tongue against hers, the hunger of someone gasping for their last breath. Lifting her hands, she brought one to his face, the other to his chest, still bare, hot now, slick from rain and sweat. There she slid around to his back and held him tighter, didn't ever want to let go.

This, she realized, was how he'd kissed her that night so long ago, when she'd invited him to Whispering Oaks to say goodbye in private. She'd brought the candles and smuggled the wine from her mother's cabinet, she'd dressed in the tight jeans and skimpy black shirt. But she'd never imagined, not once, that Jack would reach for her, that their mouths would meet and everything else would fall away, that he'd pull her close and hold her, crush her mouth with his own as if one taste would never, ever be enough.

But he had, and he did now, he kissed her like the boy he'd been, the hero she'd once worshipped, the man he insisted no longer existed. The feel of his hand along the side of her face, the whiskers scraping her cheek and her jaw, blanked her mind. And when Beauregard squirmed from between them and she found herself in Jack's lap, when she felt the ridge pressing up between her legs, something inside her shattered.

Chapter 11

She could have been hurt. She could have been—

Jack pulled Camille closer and stabbed his fingers into her hair, knew that he could never get close enough. Marcel Lambert had been there. He'd gotten to Jack, leaving Camille alone. With that man. Susan would have—

It didn't matter what Susan would have done, because Susan was not Camille, Camille who'd seen her father gunned down, who'd been pursued like an animal. Who'd stared at Jack when he'd found her, who'd lifted her arms to him and let him hold her…

Something primal swam through him as he felt her rock against him, as his own body bucked in response. Their mouths clashed; their hands roamed. Carefully he pulled her back with him, until her body sprawled over his, much like in the bathtub.

She'd faced down Lambert. She'd done as he'd asked, had found the map and surrendered it to him—the map she'd returned to Louisiana to find, the map she was convinced would lead to something of significance. She'd given it to Lambert, just handed it over.

Because of Jack...

"*'Tite chat...*" He curled his thighs around hers and held her, squeezed his eyes shut, but could still see her in the small bathtub, straddling him, gazing down with eyes huge and dark and...damaged, the way she'd looked at him all those years before.

The way she looked at him in his dreams.

What's a 'tite chat? The question had been innocent, not all that concerned. Because Susan hadn't known. She hadn't understood. She'd had no way to know her husband had been searching for another woman in the depths of his sleep, that as he'd reached for his wife, he'd wanted another.

"Jacques..." His name was thick on Camille's voice, allowing a trace of the old Cami to slip through, of the heritage she'd scrubbed away when she became Cameron Monroe. "I never stopped—"

"Sh-h-h," he murmured against her open mouth, then closed the distance between them and kissed her again. Kissed her deeper. Harder.

This, he knew. This was how he'd kissed her then, that long-ago night he'd never been able to scour from his mind, no matter how hard he'd tried. She was Gabe's little sister. She was damaged, spinning out of control. He'd promised to protect her, to be there for her....

She's messed up, frère. *She's hurtin' real bad.*

I'm not gonna let anyone hurt her, Jack had promised

his friend. *If anyone so much as looks at her the wrong way—*

But in the end it was Jack who'd looked at her the wrong way, Jack who'd crossed lines he'd considered inviolable. Gabe had been away at college. He'd trusted Jack, had trusted him to take care of his sister. Jack had promised....

"Don't let go," she whispered against his mouth. "Please don't let go."

He didn't want to. He didn't want to now and despite the frayed edges inside him, the knowledge of how dangerous her need to rock the boat was, he hadn't wanted to before. He'd opened his eyes and pulled her closer, had felt his body ready. Then she'd whispered his name.

"Jacques…"

It had all twisted, jumbled. He'd pulled back and looked down at her—

"Jack! Camille!"

Now it all shattered. Camille froze, hung that way a damning moment as Beauregard surged to his feet with a vicious little bark.

"Answer me!"

Her eyes darkened. "It's D'Ambrosia."

He looked at her sprawled on top of him, her hair tangled, her mouth swollen, her chin raw from his whiskers. Her clothes—

Another few minutes and they would have been off.

"Jack!"

Swearing softly, he eased her from his body and stood, rearranged his baggy shorts as he strode toward the creek. Beauregard darted in front of him.

D'Ambrosia broke from the cypress and ran toward the water. Russ sprinted behind him.

Camille came up behind Jack and slipped her muddied hand into his, waited quietly while her cousin's fiancé waded through the creek.

"He never left his house."

The words came at Camille through a tunnel of time and space. She tried to shake them off, but beneath the canopy of an old oak, there was no escaping what the detective was saying.

"I've got someone on him 24/7. Lambert was there last night and he's been there all day."

"Then he hired someone," Jack said. Gone was the man who'd pulled her against his body, who'd slanted his mouth against hers as if he meant to consume her. As if he *needed* to consume her.

Jacques Savoie was all business now. All sheriff.

But his mouth...his mouth was still swollen, and a small scratch streaked like a tattoo against the side of his neck. "The coward is letting someone else—"

"No." Camille looked from her cousin's fiancé to Jack. "It was *him*." Those eyes...dark and disturbing, desperate...she'd know them anywhere, had seen them too many times in the shadows of her dreams.

D'Ambrosia shook his head. "Sweetheart, I'm afraid that's just not possible."

Everything tilted, blurred. She blinked against the rain and looked at them, D'Ambrosia in his cargo pants and T-shirt, Jack wearing only gray athletic shorts, the two of them huddled around her the way Jack and Gabe had been that long-ago morning.

That man! He killed my daddy.

Petite ange. That had been Uncle Edouard. He'd

always called her his little angel. He'd gone down on one knee and lifted a hand to her face. *There was no man.*

Yes, there was. I saw him! He'd chased her.

But the rain, more than five hard, driving inches in one night, had washed away any trace of footsteps. Even hers.

Darlin'... Gabe had been soaked, covered in mud. He'd joined his uncle on his knees, had taken her hand and squeezed. *I'm afraid that's impossible....*

Then she'd been a child. She'd been young, scared. Easily manipulated. She looked at them now, at Jack and the detective, at Russ standing a few feet away, his shoulder holster visible as he talked quietly into his mobile phone.

I'm not awaiting trial....

The words nagged at her, nudged against all those fractured pieces that refused to fit together.

"We have to go," she said, standing. And Beauregard whimpered. "We have to get there before he does."

Jack's eyes, normally such a steady, emotionless brown, flickered. He stood and reached for her, pulled back at the last minute. But she saw it in his expression, the aware-ness...the memory of those broken moments alongside the creek, before D'Ambrosia's voice had cut through the wind.

"Camille—"

"Don't you see? Don't you get it?" She was tired of being treated like a child. "Lambert said the stained glass was destroyed. He said it's gone. But if that's true, why would anyone go to all this trouble to steal the map?" She'd been followed from the moment she arrived in town. "And who else?" she asked. "Who besides Lambert even knows about it?"

The answer burned: She knew. Jack knew. Saura and D'Ambrosia did. But no one else, not her mother, not even her uncles…

"She has a point," D'Ambrosia said.

But Jack's expression tightened. "Games—"

"Maybe, but that's not a chance we can take."

Russ flipped his phone shut, turned and joined them. "There's no trace of anyone," he said. "Whoever broke in made a clean getaway."

With a slow smile, Camille stepped into the center of the three men, looked first at D'Ambrosia, then at Jack— and felt the fissure clear to her bone. "But the map is worthless if you don't know where to start looking…."

She had pictures. She'd stood there on the side of the highway with her back to him, had snapped pictures of her father's map with a camera so small Jack had never even suspected. He wanted to be angry with her for that. He wanted to be angry at the secrets she'd kept—secrets that still haunted her eyes.

But he watched her walk across on the sugary-white beach of Isle Dernier, with her face lifted toward the brutally blue late-morning sky and the southerly breeze whipping her hair, and knew she'd been punished enough.

She'd lost her father. She'd lost her childhood. She'd turned her back on it all—the memories and the horror, the remnants of all those broken dreams, the ugliness and the betrayals, the sins of that long-ago storm—and forged a new life. She could have lived quietly. But she'd stepped back into a world of violence and done everything in her power to right as many wrongs as she could.

I write their stories…for those who suffered…I make sure they're remembered. I make sure no one forgets….

And now she was back in Louisiana, knee-deep in the worst nightmare of her life. She'd left a girl, a wild, reckless child; but she'd come home a woman. And this time she demanded to be heard. She had a voice now, and an audience.

God help anyone who got in her way.

Not trusting himself to watch her one second longer, Jack lowered his backpack and turned toward a fleet of shrimp boats making its way toward the barrier island. Once barely more than a forgotten sandbar, Isle Dernier was on its way back.

Lifting a hand to block the sun, Jack scanned the sparsely vegetated sand dunes and slash pines—all that remained standing on the south end of the island. New trees had been planted, but it would be another lifetime before they stood as tall as those Katrina had taken.

"Savoie," he answered when his phone rang sometime later.

"Anything yet?" Saura wanted to know.

"Not yet." The ferry had dropped them off thirty minutes before. Camille had insisted they come to the beach, rather than the Trade Winds resort where they'd booked rooms for the night. Ferry service was spotty. It was unlikely they would make the last boat back. "Anything on that end?"

"Lambert's eating breakfast." One of Camille's cousins, Cain, a former cop, was watching him. "No one has shown up for the next ferry, either." That's where Saura was, at the dock where the ferry would leave for Isle Dernier again in twenty minutes, at noon.

It was the only point of access to the small island forty miles off the coast.

And after noon, there was only one more trip south. Three o'clock sharp was the last time of return.

"And John?" Saura asked.

Jack pivoted toward a wind-bent oak, silhouetted by the sun high overhead. "In position."

It was the only way Jack had been willing to let Camille travel to Isle Dernier. Even still, with every precaution in place, unease bled through him. He had everything under control, but it only took one variable—

One freaking roadside bomb. One freaking improvised explosive device, put together in a tent or a cave somewhere…

Over. Everything. In the blink of an eye.

But the map was Camille's, and it was her father who'd been killed that long-ago night. She was the one who'd come back. She was the one who had demons to destroy….

Sliding his sunglasses to the top of his head, Jack skimmed a hand along his service revolver. "I'll call you in thirty."

The sight of Camille walking along the water's edge…

The cop in him took over, the soldier, the man who knew they were here for a reason, and that reason was not strolls down windswept beaches—or memory lane.

But it wasn't memories that tugged him toward her, wasn't memories that wound through his chest—and tightened. Pausing, she shielded her eyes and looked toward the shrimp boats. By late afternoon the gulf would consume the strip of sand on which she stood, again concealing its secrets. But now…

"Come on," he said, nearing her. "We need to go."

She turned toward him, swiping at the hair blowing against her face. "Did you and Susan ever come here?"

It was a simple question. But it cut into Jack like shrapnel. Somehow he didn't stagger back. Against the spray of the Gulf and the sand, he held himself very still, didn't trust himself to move. "No."

"Tell me," she said. "Please." Her voice barely registered above the droning, the one that wore on and on, that grew louder, would never quiet.

He looked down at her, realized how damn easily he could drown.

"About Susan," she went on when the wind kept lashing and he said nothing. "Why you pretend she didn't exist."

The acid burn consumed more. "Is that what you think I'm doing?" His voice was low, deliberately quiet. It was the voice of the soldier, the cop. Not of the son—and never of the husband. "Pretending Susan didn't exist?"

"She was your wife," Camille pushed. "You loved her. Losing her—"

He turned to the shrimp boats. "I found her," he said into the wind. "Did you know that?"

Camille stepped closer. "Saura told me."

"I found her there in the rain." The words were as stripped of emotion as the memory.

"I know."

"She'd been drinking." He'd smelled the alcohol on her clothes, found the empty wine bottle beside the bathtub. "Did Saura tell you that?"

When Camille said nothing, he looked at her, found her staring at the surf.

Her silence gave him his answer. "Did Saura tell you why?"

She glanced up, said nothing.

"She wasn't strong like you," he said, but hadn't realized the truth until too late. They'd met at a club. Dark haired and dark eyed, she'd reminded him nothing of—

In the beginning, that had been part of the appeal. "She tried," he said. "At first. But after 9/11—"

"Things got real," she finished for him.

Susan hadn't liked real. "We were in Nevada." Instantly he'd known the cozy life they'd been leading was about to go up in flames. An attack on United States soil was a declaration of war. "I'd come home and find her with a glass of wine—" Sometimes she'd been dressed. Lots of times she hadn't been. But he hadn't thought much of it, not even the drinking. Susan had always bucked traditional roles. She'd loved to be daring, shocking, to keep him guessing....

"A lot of people drink wine in the evenings," Camille said.

Jack watched a gull soar in a circle, then dip toward the water. "When I got activated, I asked her to wait here...in Louisiana." He'd liked the thought of that. He'd bought the land, had been working on the house.

"Home," Camille said quietly.

"Mine," Jack corrected. "Not hers." Half a world away, facing life and death on a minute-by-minute clock, he'd thought only of freedom, never realizing Susan viewed her time in Bayou d'Espere as being locked away, that there'd been weeks when she hadn't left the house, that she'd sat on the sofa with her wine....

Katrina had been the final straw.

"By the time I got back it was like coming home to a stranger."

Camille said nothing. As the wind lashed at them, she slowly lifted a hand to his back.

"She wanted to leave." The words chafed on the way out—in the months since he'd buried the woman he'd once vowed to love and protect, he'd not spoken of her to anyone. "Wanted to go somewhere more exciting." He could still see her sitting at the computer, pulling up travel packages. Still see the boxes that had started coming in of trendy resort wear. Sometimes she'd have it on when he got home.

"But you needed to be here," Camille said quietly. "To heal."

All those fragments, the ones he'd shoved as far and deep as possible, started to slink up.

"She didn't want me to run for sheriff. She wanted me to…" One night she greeted him in a silk robe he'd never seen before, with her hair twisted behind her head and her lipstick smeared, a crystal goblet in her hand.

It was the first time he'd wondered just what Susan did all day long, while he was in town.

"She finagled a job for me." Had been ordering him clothes, suits and ties, Italian leather loafers… "In Boston. A friend of hers lived there—her husband's family owned a bank. Susan wanted me to become a financial planner."

The light in Camille's eyes dimmed. "She didn't know you then."

"I told her no. We argued. I left."

Off the Gulf the wind pushed hard. "It wasn't your fault."

The words fell around him like a goddamned benediction. "Five weeks after I became sheriff, I was driving home. It was late. I'd been calling the house, her cell, but she never answered. I was angry, tired of living like strangers—she wanted a divorce."

Camille closed her eyes, opened them a heartbeat later.

"It was foggy." He'd been driving fast, focused on what needed to be said. "I saw the light, wasn't sure what it was." Kids, he'd thought, pulled off the road, making out in the backseat. "I stopped and got out—" The memory cut as a wave swirled around their ankles.

"And saw the blue." The fender of the convertible he'd bought for her before leaving for Iraq. "And the license tag."

The quiet knowing in Camille's eyes slipped like a buffer against all those sharp edges.

"I think I ran," he said, but didn't let himself move. He just kept staring at Camille, at those freckles bridging her nose, as the memory played in the same slow, relentless speed of the IED that ended his Air Force career. "Her eyes were open." Vacant. The car wrapped around a tree. "But she was already cold."

Camille stepped closer.

He looked down at her and lifted his hand, swiped the hair back. Lingered. "She never belonged here," he said. On Isle Dernier, with her feet ankle deep in the surf, the sun beating down and the wind swirling. In Louisiana—his life. He should have let go, should have steered clear the second he'd realized her girl-next-door smile concealed a restlessness—

Pushing up on her toes, Camille cradled his face. But he jerked away, pulled it all back into focus.

"Sins of the storm," he said like a son of a bitch, and the hard, rough edge to his voice killed the warmth in her eyes. "You sure have come to the right place, *cher*."

"Jack." The quiet knowing in her voice stripped him bare. "My book isn't about you."

A rough sound broke from his throat. He turned and reached for his backpack, slung it over his shoulder. "Keep it that way."

Time moved forward. Camille knew that. But with every step along the sandy weed-tangled path, she walked back through the miles and years and heartaches, the lies and the secrets, toward the one dream that had never died.

Her father's.

All his life he'd searched, believed. As a child, she'd been fascinated by his stories of the mystical stained glass, the way his face had glowed when he talked about barren women who could suddenly conceive, the preacher struck by consumption suddenly healthy, a cripple who could walk. All because they'd been touched by the light of the sun, filtered through an intricate depiction of the rapture, crafted by an artisan over five hundred years before. But not just any day. The magic, the miracles, came only on the summer and winter solstices.

"This way," she said. Behind her Jack walked, dark sunglasses over his eyes, the service revolver in his hand. There'd been no words in the hour since they left the beach. But she could feel him, his unease, feel him watching—retreating second by second, much like the surf pulling back from the shore.

Sins of the storms…you've come to the right place, cher.

The words kept right on whispering through her. She'd listened, had wanted so badly to help him past the pain, the guilt, to reach out and touch….

Except Sheriff Jack Savoie, abandoned son, former Air Force pilot, widower, didn't want anyone to touch him.

Especially not Camille.

If we were really strangers…we'd be in my bed. Naked.

Because then it wouldn't matter. A stranger could touch without touching. Take without giving. He could be with a stranger, and still be alone.

The small clearing stopped her. She stood inside a circle of bramble where the remains of an old cottage had almost been lost to time. Only a crumbling brick chimney jutted up from the sand like some kind of forgotten place-holder.

"My God…" Her heart started to pound. "I…remember."

Jack closed in behind her. "What? What do you remember?"

She stepped from him, moved toward the chimney. "The last time Daddy brought me here…just before he died." They'd picnicked inside the remains of the house. She'd eaten a shrimp po'boy then stretched out on a beach towel and fallen asleep.

"He brought you here?"

The sun glared hotter, but cold bled from the inside. "Yes."

Her father had been *here,* at the spot on the map he'd marked with a red star. He'd been here less than two weeks before Lambert killed him.

Going down to her knees, she lifted her hands to the bricks and ran them along the surface, worn smooth by time and wind and sand. "It can't be...."

Jack squatted next to her, kept his body between hers and the exposed area behind them. A hundred feet back, Detective D'Ambrosia kept watch.

It seemed like a lifetime ago that she'd opened the box her mother had sent her, when she'd pulled out the last stuffed animal her father had given her—a fluffy lamb, still pristine other than its yellowed fur. She'd gone through the books page by page—and found the safe-deposit box number. And the hope, the dreams that had lain dormant all those years, had burst through her. She'd known what she had to do, what her father had wanted her to do.

Now, fingers sliding against a seam in the bricks, she pulled a loose brick from the chimney—and stared at the chamber.

Crowding in behind her, Jack let out a rough breath. *"Mon Dieu."*

Her hands wanted to shake, but she would not let them. She reached for the metal box tucked inside the vault.

But even before the sun caught on the padlock hanging open, she knew what she would find.

Chapter 12

"I'm too late."

He'd told her. He'd tried to warn her. The evidence was irrefutable. Shattered glass had been found on the floor of her father's study the night he'd been killed.

No one had known its significance at the time. The pieces had been swept up and held as evidence until the sheriff had determined they had no significance.

Marcel Lambert had admitted as much to Gabe. Troy Fontenot had found the stained glass, but instead of sharing the finding with his financial backers, the Lambert brothers, he'd tried to hide his discovery.

"He found it…he had it all along."

The words were quiet, barely audible above the roar of the Gulf. But they came at Jack like a broken shout.

And he could no more kneel there and pretend she was a stranger than he could turn back time and take away all the hurt, the pain. The dreams that had refused to die, that crumbled now at the base of the old brick chimney.

She moved so fast she was gone before he could stop her. She pushed to her feet and held up the metal box, hurled it across the clearing. "How could he?" she shouted against the wind. "How could he betray—"

Jack caught her and held her, held on tight as all those walls she'd erected around the past splintered, and the grief broke free.

"It was his fault," she murmured against Jack's shirt. "He betrayed them. He stole the stained glass—"

"Sh-h-h…" Jack stabbed his hands into her hair and stroked. "He was a good man. I'm sure he never meant—"

She pulled back and glared at him. "He *lied,*" she said. "He lied to his partners. And he lied to *us*…his family."

And because of that, because Troy Fontenot had tried to bend fate to his own will, he'd died.

And Camille's childhood had shattered.

Her hands curled into tight fists. "None of it had to happen," she snapped. "*None of it!* If he'd just been honest. If he hadn't been so obsessed—"

The disillusionment…the betrayal in her voice, cut to the bone. One lie. One little sin of omission…

"Do you think your father knew?" Something shifted in her eyes, betrayal giving way to horror. "Do you think Gator knew Daddy found the Rapture, that he tried to stop him, that that's why—"

"No." The word ripped out of Jack. "You can't go there, Camille…there's no way to know."

"But what if he found out? What if your father tried to stop mine…?" Dread darkened her eyes. "What if my daddy stopped him first?"

It wasn't possible. That Jack knew for fact. Gator Savoie had been the town drunk. Everyone knew that. He'd called himself a dreamer, but the correct word had been delusional. Opportunistic.

He'd befriended Troy Fontenot at a poker game, and from that moment forward had talked of little besides the legend of the stained glass window.

If Troy had recovered the artifact, if Troy had schemed to swindle the Lambert brothers, Gator would not have stopped him.

He would have led the charge.

Gator was as dead as Troy was. He'd walked out of a bar that night, had left his family behind. And he'd never looked back. Time had gone by. They'd survived. Even Jack's mother had moved on, had finally remarried…the surgeon who'd treated her breast cancer.

But damn it, long after they made their way from the far side of the island to the hotel, Jack stood on a balcony overlooking the Gulf of Mexico—and wouldn't let himself move. Didn't trust himself to. The memories boiled too close to the surface.

Beyond, the sun slipped low against the horizon, leaving a blood-red bath in its wake, while the lights of a fleet of shrimp boats faded into the night. And from inside the posh hotel room, the hum of the shower barely registered over the rush of the wind.

Room service had come. A rolling cart covered in a pressed white cloth sat in the main room, two silver domes concealing the lobster. There was a bucket with ice in it, a bottle of premium champagne.

The water shut off, leaving only the wind and the surf. Jack curled his hands around the rail, kept his eyes on the Gulf. D'Ambrosia had taken a room, too, but the detective wasn't a man to sit on the couch and watch TV. He was casing the hotel even now, looking. Watching. Saura remained at the dock. Camille's cousin continued her vigil on Lambert. Everything was quiet. There was no sign of trouble. And yet...

Jack slid his hand to his Glock.

"Amazing, isn't it?"

He braced himself before he turned, felt the impact slam through him anyway. She stood inside the sliding-glass door, with her wet hair slicked back from her face, a thick white robe tied securely around her waist—but gaping at her chest. The decorative lights strung along the balcony illuminated the freckles.

"It's hard to look away," he said with an honesty that scraped, even as it fed some dark place deep inside.

She moved quietly, stepped around a hanging basket and joined him at the edge, bringing with her the scent of lavender and soap, of woman. "Don't get me wrong, the Pacific is gorgeous." She put her hands to the rail and leaned forward, closed her eyes and inhaled. "But it's not home."

And this was. Louisiana was. Here on Isle Dernier, where she and her father had picnicked before his death, this was home. It was in her blood, could never be washed away.

"I used to think about you," she said quietly. "When I'd watch the news and see footage from Afghanistan or

Iraq, of all the sand and flatness, never a single tree…I used to wonder if you were there…"

His grip on the rail tightened.

"And I hated it." This time her voice broke on the words. "Hated thinking of you so far away from everything you loved. Hated wondering…not knowing…every time I heard a news report about a soldier killed, a plane down—"

The words fell into silence, but he heard, and he knew. And it slayed him, slayed him to hear her admit, finally, that she'd not erased him completely from her life.

"I'm glad you're back," she said, and then her hand, with all its softness and warmth, was on his. "I'm glad you're safe."

Safe. It was a nice word, but it stabbed through him anyway.

From the grounds below, music drifted. Jazz, he thought, glancing down toward the gardens, but seeing nothing, only darkness. "We looked for you." The words tore from him. "Your family—"

"I know."

He pulled his hand from beneath hers and stepped back, pivoted toward her. "No. I don't think you do. They were worried sick, Camille. They thought—" The memory twisted hard, shoving him back in time fourteen years. "We all did."

She didn't move, other than the breeze playing with the ends of her damp hair. But her eyes were fixed on his, and they glowed. "What, Jack? What did you think?"

He wanted to look away. Christ, the only thing he wanted more than to look away, was to crush the distance between them and touch. He'd left her that long-ago morning, sitting naked and wrapped in a quilt, with no more than a kiss to her forehead and an apology. "Do you have any idea—" He bit the question back, took a hard, sharp detour. "How could you do it, Camille? To your mama, to Gabe? Hadn't they been through enough? Couldn't you have at least called, told them you were okay?"

That she wasn't hurt.

Wasn't dead.

The soft glow in her eyes dimmed, but she still said nothing. Just stared at him. As if he'd just put a knife to her gut, and twisted.

"Gabe called," he said, and it all twisted harder. Tighter. "I was in San Antonio, at Lackland. It was three in the morning." Seven minutes past three. "He was…" Jack had known the second he'd heard the panicked rasp. "You'd been missing twenty-four hours." There'd been no note, no signs of a struggle. "He told me you were supposed to be in New Orleans with Saura. That you never showed."

Camille squeezed her eyes shut, opened them a long moment later. Slowly she lifted a hand to her chest, where the robe gaped open, and rubbed.

"I wanted to leave…I wanted to help them look for you." He'd never felt so helpless in his life. Or so guilty. He'd been in Basic Training. Leave had been out of the question. He'd been forced to wait for Gabe's updates— and to let his imagination fill in the blanks.

"Do you have any idea what I thought?" This time the words perforated the darkness, the numbness, all those layers he'd slapped one on top of the other, first when his dad left, then Camille. Then in Iraq. Kneeling in the rain, holding Susan's body. Thicker and deeper, until he could breathe again. Until he could roll out of bed and not reach for a bottle.

Until he didn't feel a goddamned thing. Didn't remember.

Didn't want.

Didn't care.

"I thought you ran away." And he'd been angry, even as the guilt had pierced. "That finally you'd spun too fast." After holding it together for so long. "That you couldn't stand to be in Bayou d'Espere." That she was hurting. Scared.

"And then, when you didn't come back, didn't call…" This time he stopped himself. This time he pulled it all back in, shoved it deep. "But you were okay," he said and felt his mouth twist into an insolent little smile. "All that time, you were okay, living it up in California, becoming Cameron Monroe."

Beneath the intimate glow of the lights strung along the balcony, Camille's eyes went horribly dark. "Jack—"

"Save it," he snapped, then because he didn't trust himself to stand there for one second longer, he turned and strode into the suite.

White. It was all white. The sofa, the carpet, the walls. The little service cart with the two silver domes. Her robe. The past, the memory. The truth…the marble wet bar where Jack stood with a tumbler in his hand and his back to Camille. He'd poured two fingers of whiskey, tossed them back. Poured two more.

Now the stillness throbbed in rhythm with the breeze.

Camille closed her eyes and inhaled a breath, counted to seven, then opened her eyes to see Jack standing in the faded blue jeans and white shirt he'd worn that morning. The sleeves were rolled up and he was barefoot, but his Glock remained shoved into its holster.

She could walk away. Camille knew that. It was the smart thing to do, what she'd promised herself from the very start. She would come back to Bayou d'Espere, immerse herself in the past, get her story, make Lambert pay. Then she'd be free. And that was all she wanted. To be in control of her own destiny. To never allow anyone to dictate to her again.

Especially Jacques Savoie.

Because he was the only one who could.

"There was nothing you could have done," she said, walking through the stillness, the quiet, until she stood directly behind him. "Nothing anyone could have done."

Against the tumbler, his fingers tightened. "So you just ran."

"No." Her throat burned on the truth. For so long there'd been only her. She'd had friends and acquaintances, but never anyone close. Never anyone who would ask too many questions, want to know more.

Never anyone who could touch.

Control.

Until the day her cousin showed up on her doorstep. The shock of seeing Saura there, with her warm knowing eyes and dark hair braided down her back, had turned everything Camille had worked to build upside down.

"I didn't run," she said, tired of it all, the lies and the games, the secrets and the sins. "And I wasn't okay."

Jack said nothing. Did nothing. He stared straight ahead as if she'd done no more than comment on the color of the walls.

White.

It was all so horribly whitewashed—*he* was so horribly whitewashed.

But then he turned, deliberately, and her breath caught. Because for the first time since that night at Whispering Oaks, his eyes were vulnerable, open. The angles of his face were tight, his unshaven jaw shadowed. His mouth a hard line. But he said nothing—he didn't need to.

The question, the need—*the dread*—reverberated through the silence.

"When I left that afternoon…" she whispered, knowing it was time for the truth.

And the fallout.

"…I had every intention of going to see Saura." She'd needed a change of venue. She'd needed to be able to turn around without slamming into memories. "But when I got to New Orleans…" She could still see the Superdome glowing in the late-afternoon sun, the Garden District, the Twin Span bridge looming over the river straight ahead. "I kept going."

Jack muttered something under his breath. Cajun, creative and—wholly untranslatable.

"I didn't know where or why." Until she got there. "Didn't stop until I got to Pensacola." It had been night. She'd driven to the beach and gotten out of her car, taken off her shoes and walked to the water's edge. "It just felt so…clean." Pure.

"And you felt dirty," Jack said quietly.

"No." It was instinct that had her reaching for his wrist, instinct that had her curving her hand around flesh and bone. "No…that's not what I meant."

"Then—"

"I could breathe there." With the cool breeze off the Gulf of Mexico, much like the one that swept across Isle Dernier. The memory of it whispered through her, bringing with it the faint scent of spice and citrus, of leather and soap and man. "I could be me," she said. "No one looked at me like I was a nutcase. No one knew…" No one called her a wild child.

"And that's not running?" Jack asked.

"No." At least she hadn't thought so at the time. "It was moving forward, taking control—"

"And running," he finished for her.

Deep inside, something started to tear. She'd been fighting it for so long, holding it all together, holding it all in, but now she let it spill. Let it bleed. She angled her chin and looked up at Jack, so tall and untouchable, as if he had a damn clue what he was talking about.

"Maybe," she conceded. "But not until Marcel Lambert made his move."

She wasn't sure what she expected. For Jack to swear or come alive, for him to reach for her and take her by the arms, fire one question after another, demand answers.

Vow vengeance.

But it wasn't for him to remain so horribly, unnaturally still, while the night pulsed and the shadows stretched.

"Marcel Lambert followed you." That was all he said, the simple, detached repetition of what she'd just told him.

"Yes."

"To Florida."

"Yes."

Finally he moved, not his body, just a dark light flashing through his eyes. "He hurt you."

It all came rushing back, everything she'd tried to ignore, to destroy. And for that one broken moment, she didn't care about being vulnerable, about carving out her own life. Didn't care about proving anything to anyone. She just wanted—

She just wanted what she'd wanted fourteen years ago, when she'd sat in the darkness of that Florida hotel room with a foul-smelling bandanna tied around her eyes, another around her mouth.

She wanted what she'd always wanted.

She wanted Jack.

"He never touched me," she said quietly. Not with his hands, or his body. Words had been enough. Photos.

Jack's nostrils flared. "*Maudit,* he—"

"Wanted me gone," she supplied. "Wanted me out of the picture."

His breath came hard now, deep. As if he'd been running. Sprinting. Tearing through the scrub and the Spanish moss… "Because you saw him kill your father."

The chill came from somewhere inside, spread with needle-fine precision. She braced against it, lifted her hands and pulled the robe tighter. "Because I was growing up. Because he feared one day people would start listening to me, paying attention. That one day I might try to get even."

The lines of Jack's face tightened.

"I didn't know it was him at first. Someone broke into my hotel room. I was blindfolded, taken away. I—"

Jack's eyes flashed.

Bottled up for so long, the words wouldn't stop. "I

didn't know where he took me…didn't know how much
time had passed."

He breathed. She knew that, saw his shoulders rise,
his chest expand. But the stillness deepened, and she saw
the soldier he'd become, the discipline he'd fine-tuned.
As a boy there'd been intensity, but it had been tempered
with the laissez-faire of the deep South.

But here, now…the laissez-faire was gone. And
finally Camille realized. Finally Camille knew why Jack
had been trying to push her away.

He wouldn't let himself move, didn't want to let
himself feel.

But he did. It resonated in his eyes, the line of his
mouth, the shadow that extended beyond his jaw. "He
drugged you."

Three words, stripped of all emotion, a statement, not
a question. "Yes."

"Fils du—"

"I don't know for how long but at some point he told me
it was time to go away. Time to stay away." That had been
fourteen years ago, before cell phones and text messaging,
PDAs, the Internet. She'd tried to get word to her family,
knew if she could just let her Uncle Edouard know…

"I was shown pictures." Could still see them in her mind,
the black-and-white photos, the grainy news footage. "Of
my mother…on a stretcher." In a hospital. Hurt. "Of Gabe
at her bedside." Of her uncle and of Saura. But never of Jack.

"The accident," he muttered.

"Was a warning," she said, "a way of showing me
what would happen if I didn't do as I was told. If I tried
to contact my family, tried to resurrect the past, to prove
Marcel Lambert—"

"Killed your father."

Emotion stabbed through her, knotted in her throat. "So yes, Jack. Call it running if you want to. Call it hiding."

In the brown of his eyes, something softened. "Camille—"

"But I did what I thought I had to do," she said. "I went away and stayed away, I became someone else—"

The stillness crumbled and he was moving toward her, reaching for her.

"But I never forgot," she said, "and I never stopped planning. That's why I became Cameron Monroe," she said as his hands closed around her arms. "That's why I immersed myself in tragedy…because I knew one day I would return, and I needed a voice when I did. I needed an audience. It was the only way I could make sure Marcel Lambert paid—"

Nothing prepared her for the low roar that broke from Jack's throat, the way he pulled her into his arms and stabbed a hand into her hair, pressed the other against her back. "Sweet Mary," he muttered. "I should have been there. I should have—"

The urge to sink against him washed through her, but she struggled back, needed to see his eyes. Needed him to see hers. "No, Jack…no. There was nothing you could have done."

All those shadows, the ones in his eyes and the ones on his heart, swirled deeper, darker. "That's not true. If we hadn't slept together you wouldn't have gone off like that. You wouldn't have been alone—"

She shook her head, felt the damp ends of her hair slip against her neck. *"No."*

"I would never have let him near you. I would—"

"No." The word was hard, emphatic. "Another time, another place. You couldn't have changed the writing on the wall," she said. "The wheels were already spinning… had been for years. It was just a matter of time until Lambert made his move."

Jack wouldn't let her go, still held her anchored against him. Maybe she should have twisted. Maybe it would have worked, maybe she could have broken the contact.

Maybe not.

But in that moment she didn't want to break anything. She wanted to…fix.

She'd trained herself not to dream. She'd trained herself not to remember, not to let the images slip through the darkness of her mind. She'd trained herself to forget, to focus on the goals that drove her.

But sometimes he'd come to her anyway. Sometimes she'd seen him as the boy he'd been, and sometimes she'd imagined him as the man he'd been destined to become. The pilot.

Especially after she'd used her research skills to confirm Captain Jacques Savoie had, in fact, been stationed in Kirkuk….

She'd seen him then, sometimes in his flight suit, sometimes laughing with fellow soldiers, but sometimes alone in the desert, with the blood-red sky behind him and the sea of sand surrounding him.

"Jack," she whispered now, and against every crumb of self-preservation, she was doing it again, reaching for him, sliding her arms around his waist and linking her hands at the small of his back, holding on…. "I don't regret anything."

Hair, darker now than it had been before—the rich color of pecans—fell against the cowlick at his forehead much as it had in her dreams.

And it was all she could do not to lift a hand, slide it back…. "There's been no one else." Not even after she knew Jack had married another. Her friends had tried to set her up, had arranged a parade of blind dates. But Camille had never let anyone in, had refused to allow anyone to distort her focus. Distract her.

"I didn't want to give myself to someone like that again," she said, even as he slid a hand along her arm and up her neck, to cup her face. "Didn't want to give them that kind of control over me."

His eyes, laser-beam intense, locked onto hers. "Is that what you thought it was, *'tite chat?*"

Above the roar of the ocean, she barely heard the question.

"Control?"

Not then. Not until later. "I loved you." After so many years of denying and pretending, saying the words was like shoving a huge rock off her heart. "With everything I had." Hero worship, Saura had called it, and maybe she'd been right. "I know you never saw me like that," she acknowledged, refusing to look away, even when the glitter in his eyes turned to more of a gleam, and her blood started to hum. "Never thought of me like that, but after Daddy died…" She closed her eyes, opened them a moment later. "I don't know how I would have made it through that without you."

His smile was slow and warm, a dark, mesmerizing curve of his mouth. "You would have."

Her heart gave an odd little thump. "I wanted so badly

for you to see me as anything other than Gabe's little sister." For him to touch her as he touched her now, with a hand to her face and a hand to her back, their bodies pressed close. "I wanted you to see me for who I was...that I was growing up."

His eyes gentled. "Camille—"

"This," she whispered, skimming her mouth against his, sliding her hands to his shoulders and holding on tight. "And this," she said with another kiss, this one harder. Longer. "It was all I wanted."

He swore softly.

"It took time," she said, still pressed up on her toes, her body against his, so close she could feel the slam of his heart, "but I taught myself to stop wanting. To stop remembering...dreaming." And then Saura had shown up on her door one impossibly gorgeous afternoon, and she knew the time for making her move against Marcel Lambert had come. "So when I came back, I didn't want to see you, Jack." But had known that she would, that their paths would cross. Their agendas would clash. "Because I didn't want to feel that way again."

His thumb skimmed the freckles across her nose. "So you broke into Whispering Oaks—" He almost sounded amused.

"I knew you wouldn't approve." And the smile simply happened, curving her mouth the way it had all those years before when he'd caught her hanging curtains in his and Gabe's fort. She'd known he would be irritated.

That had been part of the fun.

"I knew you'd want to stop me." He'd always tried to do that. As a foolish teenage girl, it had struck her as impossibly heroic.

As a woman, she'd recognized the rigid edges of control.

"And I couldn't let you do that." Couldn't let anyone do that. "I'd already lost fourteen years," she said as he brushed back a few strands of hair that had fallen against her face. "*Fourteen years* because of Marcel Lambert. I wasn't willing to lose a single second more."

He smoothed the damp strands back, left nothing between them but the raw, naked truth. "And you thought I'd do that."

"It's exactly what you tried to do." And she'd been so determined to defy him that she'd never let herself look more closely, to see the demons that drove him.

"All I could think was that I had to stop you from stopping me, even if that meant treating you like you were the enemy." A stranger. A man with whom she shared nothing...wanted nothing.

"That's why I didn't tell you everything." Why she'd told lies and kept secrets, why she'd forced his hand: to make sure the softness didn't come back, the wanting didn't start all over again.

"I tried to be Cameron Monroe. I tried to be a stranger, to look at you and not see, not remember." Not want. "But I couldn't do it, Jack. I didn't know how to leave you alone, not when I could tell you were hurting."

Didn't know how to leave him alone, even now, when survival instincts demanded that she walk away.

"I tried to ignore the shadows in your eyes, to keep it all business. I told myself you didn't need me...."

Against her bottom lip, his thumb stilled. "So goddamned brave—"

"I told myself you were broken, that you didn't want to be fixed. That's why you looked at me with those flat eyes." Why he'd been so detached. "And I thought that by being someone different, treating you like *you* were someone different, I'd create distance…that I wouldn't be vulnerable." Because a stranger wouldn't care. A stranger wouldn't try to reach him.

A stranger couldn't touch.

But it was he who touched now. "That's not what you created."

Wrapped in the thick terry cloth robe, with her legs bare and the warm breeze swirling around her legs, she finally realized the truth: her plan had backfired.

"No," she whispered. Without the ties that bound them, the lines that had once defined them, without the shadows that haunted, even now, there'd been only heat. "You were the only one," she told him. "The only one who could derail me."

Make her want—make her bleed.

His eyes almost seemed to glow. "Protect you."

She tried to back away. Couldn't.

Tried to slip back into the role of Cameron Monroe—couldn't do that, either.

"When I heard you go down in the bathroom…" Even now, the memory of that sickening thud chilled her to the bone. "I knew you were in there, that you were hurt—"

He pulled her closer, tangled his hand in her hair.

"—and none of it mattered…nothing did. Not the book or Marcel Lambert, not the revenge I'd craved for so long. Because you were hurt and all I could think—"

The glitter in his eyes killed her words. Everything else faded, leaving only the relentless pounding of her heart—and the way Jack looked at her, the way he stood so horribly still, as if he didn't trust himself to let go, to move…to so much as breathe.

But then his hand shifted and his fingers found her mouth, pressed. "Don't."

Chapter 13

Shadows slipped and fell, pushed in from all directions. But they didn't touch Camille. She remained only inches away, her eyes wide—glowing, damn it. Her eyes glowed with a promise that damn near gutted him.

He'd thought her dead. He'd thought something horrible had happened to her. That had been the only way to explain her disappearance. The Camille he'd known— the Camille he'd loved—would never have abandoned her family.

But then he'd crept through the darkness of Whispering Oaks and found her, caught her going through one of the crates he'd left out as bait. With her hands to the wall, she'd slowly turned to him.

We all have choices, Jacques. Isn't that what you always said?

Now the bulky white robe served as a sharp contrast

to the angle of her jaw. She studied him through those amazing eyes. Waiting. And all Jack could think—

He wanted to touch. He wanted to drink. Christ, he wanted to drown. She'd walked away from everything, had given up the life she loved, to keep her family safe.

The tightness in his chest spread with insidious force. Lambert would pay for what he'd done to her, what he'd done to them all. He'd pay for what he'd cost her, what he'd taken from her.

For what he'd taken from Jack.

Slowly he let himself step closer. "Last night," he said, careful to keep his voice nice and slow, steady, "I told you that men like me don't make love to women like you."

He wasn't sure what he was expecting, but it wasn't for her eyes to gleam. "And then you walked away," she said. "Without answering my question."

The need to touch collided with the need to protect. "I didn't think I needed to."

Her smile widened. "Didn't think you needed to…or knew I wouldn't believe you?"

From beyond the balcony, a boat horn sounded. "I've seen things," he told her. "Done things—"

"No." She rested her hand on his jaw. Slid her fingers along the whiskers he hadn't shaved since she'd walked back into his world. "That's not what this is about."

He stiffened.

"You've *lost* things," she corrected in that steady voice of hers, the one that soothed, even as it lashed. "That's what this is about. You've lost…and you don't want to lose anymore."

The words, the truth, came at him like a quick punch to the gut.

"But tell me something." Feathering her fingers higher on his face, she slid her thumb along his cheekbone. "What exactly were you trying to warn me about?" Light played against her face, but the gloom pushed closer. "That when a man like you takes a woman like me to bed it's not making love? That it's crude and base…meaningless…."

The image formed before he could stop it, of her naked and beneath him—on top of him. Sliding against him. Of her hair spilling against him, her mouth slanting against his, giving and taking, demanding; her body soft and warm and—

"Or that a man like you," she continued, raising to her toes and never looking away, never hesitating, bolder now than she'd been all those years ago, "doesn't let himself anywhere near a woman like me?"

It all started to crumble then, to blur, all those hard dark lines he'd drawn, the need to touch and the need to protect, leaving only a boiling urgency that incinerated everything but the truth.

"I didn't want you to be Camille," he said hoarsely. She'd given him the truth, damn it, every raw piece of it. She deserved the same. "I wanted you to be this reckless, irresponsible stranger."

Her gaze met his. And slowly she stepped away.

He wanted to bring her back.

"Because then you wouldn't care what happened to me," she whispered with no accusation in her voice. No recrimination. "Is that still what you want?"

He stepped toward her, stopped when she lifted her hands to the sash at her robe.

"That if you touch me," she said, "if I touch you—"

with a quick flick the sash fell away and the robe fell open "—that it means nothing?"

Before there'd been shadows. Now the soft glow of the lamplight played against the curve of her waist and the swell of her hips. "No," he rasped, or at least he thought he did. It might have been a strangled sound. He wasn't sure. Didn't know. Didn't much care.

"Everything," she said in that same soft, steady voice, the one that fed that broken place inside him. Then she was moving toward him and putting her hands on the buttons of his shirt. "That's what it means to me." The top button flicked open, then the next, the next, until his shirt hung open and she smoothed her hands against his chest. "Everything."

One step. That's all he needed to take. One little step. Toward her. To slide the robe from her shoulders, to let it puddle at her feet. One step to pull her into his arms. One step to taste and touch—

But he did not let himself move. Because once he started—

He was a man who liked it nice and slow…but there was nothing nice or slow about Camille Rose Fontenot. Not before—not now. She'd always reminded him of one of those storms that blew up in the afternoon, wild and dangerous, but beautiful, evocative. Unpredictable. He never knew when she would strike, how she would strike—if she would strike.

Never knew what would be left standing in her wake.

When he looked at her, something inside him went a little crazy. And the tighter he held, the more he tried to control, the more it all spun away from him.

"Camille, I never meant to—" But then she slid her

mouth along one flat nipple, used her tongue to flick and tease, and he couldn't do it anymore, couldn't pretend he didn't want her, that he hadn't wanted her since the moment he'd found her at Whispering Oaks.

Long, long before that.

Need blanked him. He took her by the arms, lifted her toward him until she looked up from his chest, looked up with her hair falling against her mouth and a low gleam in the blue of her eyes.

"You make me crazy," he muttered, but didn't fight it anymore, not as she smiled a lazy smile.

"And that's not what you want?" she whispered. His mouth slanted against hers with an urgency that rocked him. She tasted of peppermint toothpaste and determination, of courage and dreams and—

Heaven help him. She tasted of salvation.

The word should have stopped him. Instead he pulled her closer, kissed her deeper. Their mouths met and clashed, demanded and took. And her body, so warm and sinuous, pressed to his. He could feel her breasts, bared by her open robe, pressed against his chest. And the need to touch them, taste them, fired through him.

"It's called a free fall," he muttered against the moist warmth of her mouth. Trying to keep it slow, to not go too fast, he eased the robe along her arms, let it fall to the floor. "When the instrument panel goes out or the engines fail…when no matter how hard you try to regain control the plane just keeps falling."

She tilted her head, gave him access to her neck, even as her hands fisted against the fabric of his shirt, and pulled.

"It's subtle at first," he murmured against her neck. "Gentle almost." He reached her collarbone as she tugged his shirt from his arms. "Because you're so damn high you barely notice." With the words he slid lower, brought his hand to the swell of her breast. "But then it accelerates, gets faster." There he flicked. "And in those last few seconds before impact—"

"I'm not going anywhere, Jack."

The promise in her voice broke through the haze, had him glancing up to find the light in her eyes.

"I'm not going anywhere," she said again, this time softer, and the vise around his chest, the one that had been constricting ever since she arrived, ratcheted even tighter.

"Yes," he said slowly, deliberately. He'd tried, damn it. He'd tried. "You are."

Her eyes darkened, but before she could voice the question, he lifted her into his arms.

Nothing prepared her. Nothing could have. Not the dreams, the memories. Nothing prepared her for the way he crushed her in his arms and strode toward the bedroom, slowly, deliberately, never looking away from her, not even to flick on a light. He just held her, and carried her, brought her to the bed and eased her down, put a knee to the mattress and went down with her.

Somewhere along the line, someone had turned down the sheets.

With a slam of her heart Camille looked up at Jack, at the slow burn in his eyes and the hair against his cowlick, his wide, flat cheekbones and full lower lip, the whiskers shadowing his jaw. And all she could think was more….

"Jack…" He braced his hands on either side of her and leaned down, but with a throaty laugh she eased him back to his knees and came up on hers. There they faced each other, and there they kneeled. There she ran her palms along the strength and the warmth of his chest.

"We've got all night," she whispered, and would have sworn she heard a ragged sound rip from his throat.

His gaze dipped, lingering on her breasts before sliding lower. He didn't touch, though, not with his hands. But she felt the kiss whisper through her blood. "So beautiful…."

Somewhere below, the waves lapped against the beach. And from the hotel grounds, music drifted. The breeze swirled warm and hypnotic as Jack's hands found her breasts and her nipples pebbled. His thumb teased and his mouth claimed. On some hazy, peripheral level Camille knew this, but as she arched into his mouth, there was only Jack.

Jacques.

And an urgency that pounded harder and faster than any hurricane ever had. Ever could.

She held on, curled her fingers into his arms, dug in as the pleasure throbbed through her. She heard the little mewl, but it took a second to realize it came from her own throat.

Mindless she twisted against him, urged him to her other breast. He slid against her, let his hands lead and tease. Then his mouth closed around her other nipple. But his hands kept going, curving around her lower back to her buttocks, where he pressed. She could feel him then, all of him, a hard ridge straining against his jeans.

Sensation pulsed like a drug. She closed her eyes and sucked in a sharp breath, hung there in the moment. *With Jack.* But then need pierced and she shimmied away, let a wicked little smile curve her mouth as he came up for air.

And when she spoke, it was more breath than voice. "My turn."

Earlier his eyes had glittered. Now they grew heavy-lidded. Camille lowered her face and claimed one flat mauve nipple. First with soft little kisses. Then an open mouth. Then her tongue. And this time she knew the low growl came from him. Driven by it, she ran her hands down his stomach to the trail of hair that led to his waistband. There, she bypassed the zipper and went lower, cupped against the rough fabric of his jeans.

He rocked against her palm, rode her as she pulled against his nipple.

Never had she imagined—never had she let herself dream. That morning when they'd left for the island she'd only allowed herself to focus on her father's map, what they might find.

Never had she considered nightfall would find her naked in Jack's arms, and that what they'd find would be each other.

She looked up at him, found his eyes closed. But his face wasn't relaxed. It was pulled tight, locked in a struggle she was only beginning to understand. He'd been holding on so tight, for so long, denying, isolated….

"Jacques." His eyes opened as she feathered her fingers along his jaw. "Let me love you," she whispered against the ache in her heart. "Let me show you—"

He moved so fast she never had a chance to finish. The chain of restraint fell away and he was there, pulling her into his arms and taking her mouth with his own, easing her down against the soft cotton of the sheets. She pulled him down with her, curved one hand around his bicep as she pushed the other into his hair, held on as he deepened the kiss, as he gave and took and demanded. She arched against him, felt the ridge, the rub of denim, against her inner thigh.

And then his hand was there, sliding along her stomach to between her legs, where he slid first one finger, then two, to find her hot and ready. He slipped inside, and for an amazing second she hung there, and savored.

But just a second. Need surged, demanded. "Please," she whispered as she caressed the warmth of his stomach to the waistband of his jeans. There she fumbled with the fly, freed him. Wasting no time she shoved against the denim as he kicked, and then he was there, all of him.

His eyes, gleaming like warm melted chocolate, met hers. "You," he whispered, sliding the hair from her face, then reaching for her hand. She put her palm to his and closed her fingers around his, smiled slowly as she opened to him, felt him settle between her legs—and push inside.

Sensation streamed, swelled. Heat curled, and need demanded. After so many years of being alone, of trying not to remember, not to want, her body accepted him, welcomed him. Held him. Fourteen years had passed since she'd last been with a man, *with this man*. Then she'd been a child, her courage manufactured through a bottle of wine. Then she'd been desperate, devastated.

Now different needs drove her, deeper, more primal. She'd tried to stay away. She'd warned herself, knew the consequences—but flat didn't care. There was only Jack and the feel of him moving inside of her, of his hand holding hers—and the reality that she never wanted him to let go.

That *she* never wanted to let go.

On a rough breath he pulled out and eased back in, rocked there, shredded what was left of her heart when he squeezed his eyes shut and threw back his head, the tight lines of his face suspended between excruciating pleasure—and even more excruciating pain.

"Love me," she murmured into the silence, the stillness—and with the quiet words it all broke, and there was no more silence. No more stillness. No faint music and no wind, only the feel of their bodies moving together.

"Love me," she whispered again, but this time without voice.

And as his eyes opened and met hers, as he drew her hand to the pillow beside her face and increased the tempo, that's exactly what he did.

He'd forgotten.

During the fourteen years since he'd last seen her, he'd forgotten what she could do to him, how quickly she could unravel him, then wind him right back up into tight, soul-shattering knots. Her smile, so wide and pure and trusting, had been enough to knock the breath from his lungs. And when she'd matured from girl into teenager, when the awkward shyness had given way to a stabbing desperation, when she'd dared him to teach her to kiss—to love...

Even then he'd known she was dangerous.

And even then he'd known he was so not the man for the job.

But then she'd been a child, and the power she'd had over him was nothing compared to the woman she'd become. She could still twist him up with just an easy pure-Cami smile, but the dark light in her eyes, the glow of horror and hope, of loss and grief and strength, of hard, gritty courage…

He looked at her now, at the warm water raining down from the shower and sluicing along her face, her chest, and damn near forgot to breathe. He'd told himself no more. He'd told himself never again.

Love me…

The words, the memory, seduced. Even as it punished. He'd been so sure he didn't know how, that there was nothing left inside of him.

"It's lavender," she said, and he blinked, brought her back into focus, saw the small bottle she'd lifted to her face. She smiled. "Big, tough, untouchable Jacques Savoie is going to smell like a *flower.*"

Lavender. Sweet mercy, lavender. The scent had haunted him. Every time he'd smelled it he'd turned, looked.

Until the one time the scent had pulled him from sleep, and he'd found his wife leaning over him, asking if he liked her new perfume….

Crushing the memory, he stepped toward Camille and joined her under the spray. "No flowers."

Her eyes, so luminous and blue and happy, dazzled. "What's the matter, Sheriff? You're not scared, are you?"

He reached for the shampoo, but she slipped her arm behind her back. "Be careful now, *cher,*" he said, and the teasing cadence to his voice rocked him. He couldn't remember…didn't have a single idea when was the last time he'd teased someone. "You sure you want to do that?"

She tilted her face. "Do what?"

The urge—*the need*—to touch drove him. He stepped toward her, felt the warm slipperiness of her legs as their bodies touched—and his readied.

"My, my," she said in that same throaty voice, playful now whereas before, in bed, there'd been only intensity. "Is that a big tube of soap you've got there, Sheriff, or are you just—"

He took her mouth before she could finish, pulled her slick body to his. She stepped into him, lifted her sudsy hands to his shoulders—and laughed.

"Gotcha," she said against his open mouth.

Leaning back, he glanced toward his shoulders, smelled before he saw. Lavender. She slid her hands down along his arms, to his stomach, lower— "Too bad it's not chocolate," she murmured as she took him in her hands and rubbed. And squeezed.

The rumble started low and built, rumbled up through his throat. He tossed his head back and tried to savor, to enjoy, but the need pushed too hard, and before he could stop himself he caught her hands and backed her toward the little white tiles, took her mouth and absorbed her laughter. And then he was pushing inside and she was welcoming him, again, and again.

And with the warm water pulsing against them, he forgot all about smelling like a flower—and never wanting again.

She loved lavender.

With the moonlight playing against them, Camille lay on her side, with a hand against Jack's stomach, watching him sleep. Finally. It had been like a game of chicken, neither wanting to drift off first. But after he'd carried her back to bed and she'd slid on top, after she'd held his hands up by the pillow as he'd let her take over, take control, after all that, when she'd lain quietly atop of him, the rhythm of his breathing had finally deepened.

Now she skimmed her fingers along his body, toying with the trail of dark hair that vanished beneath the sheet at his hips. She didn't want to wake him, not when for the first time since she'd come home, the shadows were gone, the lines of his face relaxed.

So she lay there and watched. Earlier there'd been music. Now the only rhythm came from the rise and fall of his chest, the steady cadence of his heart. She wasn't sure how much time passed…somewhere along the line the bedside clock had hit the floor. The low rumble of thunder came first, through the window the occasional flicker of lightning. Then the patter of rain. Hearing a soft flapping from the outer room, she slid from bed and felt the chill, grabbed the big towel from the floor. She wrapped it around her and padded from the bedroom, stepped into the living area, where the two silver domes still sat atop the white-cloth-covered serving tray. When Jack awoke, maybe they could—

The movement came through her peripheral vision. She spun toward her left—and saw him. He stood just inside the sliding-glass door with Jack's backpack in his hands. And in that horrible frozen moment, everything flashed. Recognition hit with brutal force. "You…"

"Easy there, sweet girl," the man said. "I'm not going to hurtcha…."

Chapter 14

The voice crawled over her. She tightened her hand against the towel and retreated, but the denial wouldn't come. "It was you," she whispered as he froze, tall and disheveled, his hair long and silver, but his eyes—God, his eyes.

They were the eyes from before, the eyes that had gleamed at her through the ski mask in Jack's house, when Jack had lain unconscious in his bathtub. The eyes of that long-ago night, that had glowed at her through the darkness before he'd lunged for her. Chased her.

The dark chocolate eyes that had glowed at her through the shadows of the bedroom, as Jack had moved over her…

"Your own son…" The words barely found voice. "You could have hurt him," she said, but deep inside, she knew that Gator Savoie already had. Brutally. He'd hurt his son in the most fundamental way imaginable, when he'd abandoned him. And now, standing there in the hotel room, with Jack's backpack in his hand, he was about to hurt him even more.

"No," he said in a rough, gravelly voice, the kind that came from too much whiskey and too many cigarettes, too much regret, from a life in ruins. "I wuz careful. I only used enough to make him sleep a little while—"

"So you could get the map." The map he and her father had allegedly used to find the depiction of the rapture.

The gravity of her mistake burned. She'd been so sure it was Marcel Lambert following her, Marcel Lambert pursuing her, that she'd never even considered other possibilities.

"I had to," Gator said. "There's been enough blood spilled already. I had to stop it, had to get that thing before anyone else found it."

"You were there that night," she whispered against the horrific chill, the one that seeped into her bones. "In my father's study. You know what happened. You—"

"No," Gator said, moving toward her, shaking his mane of silver hair. "That's not the way it was. I'd just gotten there, heard the gunshot…but then I saw you, I saw you hunched in the shadows and I knew. If Lambert saw you—"

She backed away. "No."

"I got you out of there, girl…the only way I could." Behind him, the wind pushed spatters of rain through the open door. "I made you run. I—"

"Fils de putain!"

Out of the darkness Jack materialized, bare-chested and barefoot, but with his jeans pulled over his legs, charging across the room and knocking aside the serving cart, plowing into his father. The two crashed hard, the older man going down on his stomach, Jack pinning him there, pressing his arms to the floor.

"Son," the older man muttered, but Jack showed no mercy.

"It was you," he seethed. "You who chased Camille—"

"I protected her!"

"You who've been following her, who stole her laptop and paid that kid to break into the bank. Who attacked her—"

"I didn't attack her!"

"—drugged me," Jack went on, and Camille's heart kept right on shattering. She stepped toward them, put a hand to Jack's back.

"Maybe we should get D'Ambrosia—"

He glanced back at her, his eyes an awful combination of shock and horror—and hurt. "Why don't you go on in the other room, *'tite chat.* Put some clothes on."

She stiffened, didn't move. "I'm not leaving you."

Something hard and jagged flickered through his gaze, but then he turned back toward his father. "We thought you were dead," he gritted out, and for the first time, emotion leaked into his voice. "Mama and I—"

Grieved.

Struggled.

"Don't y'think I know that?" Gator twisted toward his son, looked up at him with the most haunted eyes Camille had ever seen. "It ate at me, boy. It ate at me to know you thought I was dead—that I walked out on you. When your mama got sick—"

A hard sound broke from Jack's throat.

"I was there," Gator said. "At the hospital. I went… and when she slept, I'd sit with her."

Camille lifted her hand to her mouth as Jack rocked back.

"But I couldn't let them know," Gator went on, and a nasty, horrible feeling bloomed in her gut. "I couldn't let Lambert know I was there or he woulda—"

Camille sank to her knees, kept her hands on Jack's back. "Let her die."

"Get back," Jack snapped, but instinct wouldn't let Camille move.

"He was paying for her treatment," Gator said. "He told me he'd take care of her, take care of you both, so long as I stayed away and forgot what I saw. But if'n I ever came back—"

"You'd regret it." Camille finished the threat for him. She looked at the broken man sprawled on the floor, his gaunt cheeks and haunted eyes, and knew. Gator Savoie had made a deal with the devil. "Jack—"

But he was already shaking his head. "No. That's bullshit. If my da—" His eyes flashed. "If Gator had something on the Lambert brothers, they would have killed him, like they did your father. They'd be crazy to let him live."

Emotion clogged her throat. She looked into Jack's eyes, felt the ache slice through her heart. "There are many ways to kill someone—not all of them leave blood on your hands."

Alive.

The word pounded through Jack. His father was—

Very slowly, very deliberately, Jack turned off the cold water and looked up at the mirror hanging above the small sink at the back of his parish station. It was an antique. Oval, framed in gaudy gold filigree. Every evening MaryAnne brought in her spray bottle and paper towels and cleaned the surface until it glistened. When she got done, there were never any streaks or smears or smudges, just a blisteringly clear sheen that hid nothing.

Not his father, Jack corrected. A father didn't let obsession blind him. A father didn't put his own desires ahead of the needs of his family.

A father didn't just…walk away.

Jack pivoted from the mirror, didn't want to see those muddy eyes one second longer. He had a job to do. A suspect to interrogate.

Not. A. Father.

"Jack—"

That was the only warning he got. The second he stepped into the cool hallway, he turned toward Camille's voice—but saw his grandmother. With Camille at her side, Ruby Rose hurried toward him. Shock hollowed out her eyes—but along with it glowed a punishing sheen of hope. She spoke rapidly, in pure undiluted Cajun, questions and confusion all rolled together.

"Gran." He reached for her, hating how frail she felt, despite the steel she showed the world. "You shouldn't be here."

"He is my son," she said, struggling from Jack's arms to look up at him. "He is my boy, *mais non?* Why would I not be here?"

Because it was too soon. Too many questions remained. Gator was a suspect. Jack was the sheriff. He had a job to do. But with his grandmother gazing up at him with those tired, love-drenched eyes—

"I want to see him."

Sins of the Storm

Jack brought her painfully thin hands to his mouth and brushed a kiss against her knuckles. "In time."

But not yet. Not until all those questions tearing through him had answers.

Camille joined them, reached for him.

He stepped back.

She lifted her eyes to him, damn near slayed him with the warm, steady understanding glowing there. "You need to listen to him," she said. "You need to hear him."

He looked at her in the fluorescent glow of the overhead light, with her tousled hair and the simple white T-shirt she'd pulled on, the well-worn jeans that hugged her hips, and for a moment the storm fell away. Leaving only her, the woman who'd put her arms around him the night before, who'd opened to him and given to him, made him want to believe the eye of the storm could last forever.

"Go to him," she said calm, quiet, steady, nice and shockingly slow. "Do what you need to do. I'll be here." She reached for his grandmother's hand. "We'll be here."

"I was in Nuevo Laredo when I heard. I'd been there a few months. Stayed in an old hotel that catered to the college crowd."

Jack stared at the man across from him, every line on his face illuminated by the harsh glare of the overhead light. There'd been lines before—but only around his mouth and at the corners of his eyes. Laugh lines, his grandmother had called them….

The deep groves carved into Gator's cheeks, across his forehead, were not from laughter.

Jack knew Nuevo Laredo—once a thriving border town, the small Mexican community, a favorite among college kids looking for prescription drugs, had fallen victim to gang violence.

"There was a TV in my room, got a few cable stations." Gator lifted his eyes, those muddy eyes against a leathery face that should not have looked the same.

But did.

"Imagine my surprise when I came out from shaving one morning and saw Lambert's picture on one of those news shows. They said he was facing murder charges… that his brother Nathan was dead."

That had been March, just before Bayou d'Espere's string of break-ins began.

"And I knew," Gator said, glancing beyond Jack to the two-way mirror. Behind it stood Hank and Russ and D'Ambrosia. They'd all volunteered to handle the interrogation.

But. Jack. Was. Sheriff.

"Their reign of terror was over," Gator said. "I could come back."

Which was exactly what he'd done. He claimed he was trying to pick up the pieces he'd abandoned two decades before, that he knew the stained glass had allegedly been destroyed, but like Camille, he didn't fully believe the claim.

That's why he tried to find the map. That's why he broke into the library and the historical society, a storage building.

"I didn't set no fires," he said. "You gotta believe me—"

Jack stood. They'd been at this over an hour. "I don't have to do anything."

"He's hurting."

"Of course he is," Saura said. She shifted the convertible into Park and turned toward Camille. "In less than a week his whole world's blown up all over again."

Camille closed her eyes, but could still see him standing in the hallway outside the interrogation room, so tall and isolated, in full cop mode. There wasn't a trace of son to him, not even in the dark brown of the eyes he'd inherited from the man on the other side of the door.

She'd waited with Ruby Rose as minutes had dragged into hours, until finally the sun had started to slip against the horizon and Ruby had started to yawn. D'Ambrosia had popped out, whispered something to Saura. A few minutes later she'd suggested they clear out for a little while, go home and clean up.

It was a nice suggestion, but Camille knew the truth.

Jack wanted to be alone.

Long after she hugged her cousin goodbye and went inside Jack's house, locked up, the ache of being shut out kept right on winding, deeper, tighter. She wanted to be there for him. She wanted to support him. But he wanted to be alone.

It was all he knew.

In the bathroom, she turned on the water. She'd shower and put some dinner on, take a few minutes to jot some notes. The book was changing. With each day in Bayou d'Espere, *Sins of the Storm* shifted, intensified. It was her story, her life, but the curveballs kept right on coming. Gator—

She closed her eyes, opened them a long moment later. All this time, he'd been alive. All this time he'd been living in exile. All this time he'd been planning his return.

Just like her.

Numbly, she pulled off her shirt and wriggled out of

her jeans, stilled when she caught sight of herself in the mirror—and everything started to blur.

Love wasn't supposed to hurt. Smiles weren't supposed to scrape. But as she lifted a hand to her chest and rubbed, all those jagged pieces inside rubbed against each other, hurting.

Love me...

She hadn't thought it possible. She'd thought Jack too broken, too isolated. That he didn't know how to love anymore. Didn't want to. That he'd been so lost in the debris of his life, that he wouldn't let himself reach out. Wouldn't let himself want.

But there in the shadows of the hotel room, he'd reached, and he'd wanted. And in response, her body still burned.

Turning from the mirror, she noticed the empty towel rack and stepped toward the linen closet, looked inside. A neat stack of blue towels sat on the bottom shelf. She reached for one, was turning toward the shower when the plastic registered. She turned back toward the bag stashed at the back of the shelf, behind the towels, and everything inside of her stopped.

Everything else, all those dreams she'd begun to let herself build, crumbled.

Through the front windows, light glowed.

Jack sat in his squad car for a long moment and watched. He'd bought this land, built the Acadian-style house almost completely by himself. For Susan, he'd told himself. He'd built the house for his wife, to make her happy.

But the plans, the dreams, had begun long, long before Susan had ever walked into his life. And she'd never been happy there, not when he'd shown her the overgrown parcel of land, not when he'd rolled out the blueprints, not when he'd blindfolded her and carried her over the threshold.

Finally he knew why. That day, when he'd carried her inside, he'd brought her into another woman's home.

And somehow she'd known it.

With the purple glow of twilight fading, he glanced at the rose bed, no longer consumed by weeds, but cleared, ready to grow.

Gator had been released. Charges were pending. There was no evidence linking him to the fires. To everything else, he'd confessed. He'd confessed, and he'd returned what he'd taken. He'd sat there in the small interrogation room, a broken man. And Jack had tried so damn hard to be the cop he'd become, but the boy had been there, the boy who'd missed his father.

I'm sorry, son...so dadgummed sorry.

There are many ways to kill someone—not all of them leave blood on your hands.

Marcel Lambert had done that. He'd killed more than just Troy Fontenot that rainy night over two decades before. He'd killed bits and pieces of them all.

Opening the car door, Jack stepped into the warmth of early evening. Less than a week had passed since he'd faced Whispering Oaks and savored the anticipation, walked through the rain. Nice. And. Slow.

Now it was all he could do not to run.

He strode toward the light glowing from the window and pulled open the screen door, slid his key into the lock and pushed inside.

The suitcase stopped him cold.

Beauregard nudged at his hand, but when Jack looked up, everything stretched and blurred. His house, he knew. It was his house, his rug and piano. The air-conditioning blew. Light shone from a single lamp.

But the children were there, in their torn clothes, playing alongside the dirt road. And the other dog, half-starved, limping. And the sun. It beat down without mercy or reprieve, glared like a spotlight. The sand stung.

But then the sting became rain, and the light slipped into darkness. And the headlights cut through the fog. And he was running, limping, going down on his knees....

Because of her eyes. She sat without moving, neatly dressed in khaki slacks and a white shirt, with her hair combed and pulled behind her face, her legs crossed, her eyes...flat. Cold.

And then he saw the map.

It sat on the old sea trunk, no longer encased in plastic, no longer hidden behind a stack of towels. It sat, and it condemned. "Camille—"

Mechanically she stood. "Do you have any idea...any idea at all what went through my mind when I heard that thud from the bathroom?"

The explosion shattered the afternoon, the smoke and the shrapnel, the brutal moment of silence, followed by cries of agony. He'd tried to run, tried to reach them, the children....

"I was scared," Camille said, but there was absolutely no emotion in the words. Her voice. "I thought you were hurt," she said with another step toward him. "I thought—" She broke off as her eyes flashed. "I didn't think twice about giving Gator the map...the map my father had left for me...*the map he'd given his life for!*"

Viciously she stopped and stripped the emotion from her voice, her face. "Because I thought you were hurt."

Everything inside Jack tightened, twisted. "I know." And God help him, his voice wasn't empty like hers, like his had been for so long. The awareness left his throat raw. "You were so damn brave—"

"Foolish," she snapped. "I fell for it, Jack...fell for it all. Like a good little puppet I did exactly as you wanted, handed over what I thought was my father's map." She grabbed it from the table and shoved it at him. "All so you could stay in control. So you could try to stop me just like you've always tried to stop me...convince me I was in danger—"

"No." With the word he moved, reached for her. "That's not what happened."

The blue of her eyes, the blue he'd damn near drowned in the night before, darkened. "No?"

"No." She stiffened when his hands found her arms, but she didn't step away. "The trap wasn't for you." She wasn't even supposed to be there. "But for him...for Gator." Only Jack hadn't known it was his own father he was trying to catch. "I brought the map home and planted a fake...but, Sweet Mary, I never meant for you to get caught in the cross fire."

Her chin came up at a fierce angle. "Because you never even planned to tell me, did you?"

The rain slashed harder, drenched him as he dragged the body into his arms and searched for a pulse. But knew he would not find one.

"I was trying to protect you—"

"*Protect* me." She spat the words at him. "Protect me with lies? Protect me by shutting me out?"

Just like you did all those years before.

She didn't say the words, didn't need to. They both knew.

"That's not protecting," she said with a deceptive quiet. "That's control."

Everything inside him stilled.

She twisted hard and stepped back, held up her hand to keep him from following. "I knew better," she said. "When I came back, when I knew I would see you…" Her eyes narrowed. "I knew you'd shut yourself off, that you were broken inside. I knew that, and I told myself to stay away. Stay clear. I told myself to be Cameron Monroe, to be a stranger, to make sure Cami Rose never surfaced. Because I knew if she did—"

It was all slipping, so hard and so fast, with the sun and the sand, the darkness and the rain, slipping and swirling. "Damn it, Cami—"

"She would see the pain," Camille said in that horrible rote voice as if she were talking about a freaking stranger, and not herself. "And she would want to help."

"She's you, *'tite chat*." No matter how badly he'd wished otherwise. He'd wanted her to be a stranger, damn it. He'd wanted her to be someone else—*anyone* else. He'd wanted to live in the moment, without all those ties that bound. Then she wouldn't have known…would never have been able to touch. "Camille…Cameron… they're both you."

"But you're not Jack," she said, lifting a hand to her chest. There, she rubbed. "The blinders are finally off. And now I can see what I wouldn't let myself see before. I don't know you anymore…you are a stranger, someone hard and isolated, who doesn't know how to live in a world where you don't control every variable." Eyes glittering, she shoved the hair from her face. "And I can't live like that."

The words seared like acid. "So you're just going to walk away." The rain kept falling, but he didn't move, not for a long, long time. "Just like you did before…find the first excuse you can and walk away."

Her eyes flashed. "I had no way of knowing—"

"That Lambert would follow you to Florida, no. But you were the one who got in that car, Camille." He could see it now, see it so damn clearly. She'd been a loose cannon since the night her father died. For years he'd tried to fix that, tried to stop her. Protect her. But she didn't want his protection. She only wanted to keep spinning, to duck out when the consequences caught up with her. "You were the one who tucked tail and ran," he said against the boil in his gut. "Who drove to Florida without telling a soul."

Maybe it was a breath…maybe it was a hard broken laugh. But the sound ripped from her throat as the light in her eyes went completely out. "There you go, Jack. Make this my fault. Do whatever you need to make yourself feel better." She managed one step before Beauregard rolled to his feet and nudged at her hand. She opened her fingers, stroked them along his ear. "I'm not going to stop you." Her eyes met his. "I can't give my heart to a man who doesn't know the difference between control and love."

The dust settled and the rain slowed, leaving only the debris. And the cold. It seeped through him one cell at a time, the insidious death he'd vowed to never feel again.

Beauregard whimpered, but Jack didn't look, just let

all those broken edges crystallize as he found the most insolent smile he could, nice—and slow. "Who said anything about love?"

Chapter 15

Before, he'd kissed her. All those years ago, that chilly morning when he'd crushed what was left of her heart, he'd slipped from her arms while she pretended to sleep and dressed, turned to her and leaned close, pressed a kiss to her forehead and told her he was sorry.

That he never should have lost control like that.

Cold and naked and refusing to shake, she'd clenched the threadbare quilt—and vowed not to break. Because finally she'd realized. Finally she knew. Jacques Savoie could not give her what she wanted.

Because even then he'd been carefully constructing his life, one steady, predictable layer at a time.

And she had not been part of his plan.

Just as she wasn't now.

All those years ago, she'd watched him walk away, hadn't moved until she heard the car engine. Then she'd gone to the balcony door and watched him drive away.

Now it was she who straightened her shoulders, she who lifted her eyes. But she didn't step toward him, didn't insult him with a kiss to the forehead. She just let her mouth flatten.

Who said anything about love? he'd asked in that empty stripped-bare voice, the one that embodied the man he'd become.

"No one," she answered. Then she tore her hand from Beauregard's silky fur and walked toward the door, opened it and stepped into the warmth of twilight, kept right on walking until she reached her rental. Saura had dropped it off earlier. Now she opened the door and slid inside, started the engine.

This time it was she who drove away, and Jack who made no move to stop her.

Through the darkness, the red glow of taillights vanished.

Jack moved from the window to the front door, pulled it open and let Beauregard bolt into the night. But Jack didn't follow, didn't move, just stood as the breeze resurrected the scent of lavender.

Resurrected. The word stabbed deep.

From the moment he'd found her snooping around Whispering Oaks, he'd known the nice and slow world he'd carefully constructed was about to shatter. Where Cami walked, trouble followed. It had been that way as long as he could—

He stopped the lie before it could form. It hadn't been that way as long as he could remember. Just since the night she'd seen her father murdered. That's when everything had changed. That's when everything had fallen apart. That's when the sweet little girl had broken, when the desperation had started. The stunts. The recklessness.

Fourteen years hadn't changed a damn thing.

Love me...

Now, Christ...the scent of lavender seared his soul.

Big, tough, untouchable Jacques Savoie is going to smell like a flower....

He never should have touched her. He never should have let himself close. Let himself touch and taste, let himself remember what it felt like to hold her. To hold on.

The need to go after her almost sent him to his knees. To find her and pull her into his arms, to destroy the hurt he'd seen glistening in her eyes. The hurt he'd put there. He wanted to tell her she was wrong, that he did know how to live in a world where he didn't control everything.

But the truth wouldn't let him move.

Looking back, it's all so clear now. At the time, everything seemed normal, full of the swirl of activities that make up our lives. But looking back, I can see it. There was nothing normal about those last few weeks before my father died. There was nothing rote or ordinary. It's almost as if...

He knew.

With the whispers of morning pushing through the curtains, Camille stared at what she'd just written.

Propped up in bed, she'd been writing for hours. Sometime after midnight, she'd tried to sleep, but the clutter in her mind wouldn't let her. She needed to get it all out, let it spill onto the paper, before the truth, the memories, ate her alive.

I know now that those last few weeks were magical, full of special times. As if my father was purposely building memories of the lifetime we would not share. There were more stories, more little gifts, more time together. I can still remember—

I.

The word stopped her. *I*. First person, not third. Everything else she'd written, every word, was from the perspective of a third-party observer. But somewhere between night and dawn, the tense had changed, and it was no longer Cameron Monroe who wrote. No longer Cameron Monroe who remembered. But Camille. Camille Rose Fontenot.

Troy's daughter.

Troy's little girl.

It all came harder then, faster, like water busting through floodgates, surging, rushing forward.

—the trip to Isle Dernier. Yes, he took me there to conceal his true objective, but it was still our time. Still magical. We fished together. He gave me the sand dollar. We shared a picnic. He held me while I napped. I don't have any pictures…but I don't need them. Because the images live inside me. All

I have to do is close my eyes and the ugliness falls away. And Daddy is there. With me. His eyes, the same shape and color as mine, warm and crinkled. I can see him as he was the very last time—

Her hand froze. The words blurred, lost form, and then there was only him, her father, standing at the top of the sweeping staircase at Whispering Oaks, counting to ten. She'd scrambled away…

Two.

…and run through the massive foyer.

Three.

…through the dining room.

Four.

…outside, around the house.

Five.

She'd wanted to stump him. She'd wanted to hide so cleverly he would give up without finding her….

Six.

She'd never heard another number. She'd crouched behind the old well and waited. And waited…

On a hard slam of her heart, Camille pushed her notebook aside and reached for her jeans, dressed, grabbed her purse and went for the door. Inside her rental she flicked the ignition and backed out, gunned the car toward the main highway. Not even the sight of Russ, watching her still, no less covertly than before, slowed her. Instead she fumbled for her cell and jabbed out Saura's number.

Jack ran. Beauregard broke through the scrub and raced toward the house first, Jack a close second. His lungs burned. His leg ached. He stopped at the porch and reached down to rub his thigh, knew it wouldn't do a damn bit of good. His doctors had warned him about that. Shrapnel wounds could heal, but the nerve damage, the pain, never fully went away.

With more of a limp than usual, he made his way up the steps and across the porch, reached for the door. He needed to—

Christ. He hated that word. *Need.* It was the one thing he'd never wanted to feel again. To want. He'd just wanted to walk through life without strings or complications, to make sure nothing ever blew up in his face again.

Even if that meant pushing away the one person who made him want...

His cell was ringing as he pushed inside. He grabbed it and checked caller ID, frowned.

"The alarm's going off," his secretary told him. "Over at Whispering Oaks."

He stilled. "You don't say?"

"You said you wanted me to let you know—"

"I know what I said." He also knew his father was still downtown. The danger, not that there'd ever really been any, had passed. And he was done chasing his tail. "Send Russ."

Camille worked her way through the old house one room at a time. Her father had had ample time. She'd been outside behind the well for a seeming eternity while he'd been inside. Alone.

He'd had more than enough time to hide the stained glass window.

All those broken misshapen pieces, the ones that had sliced so badly in the weeks and months after her father's death, the ones that had seemed disjointed and unimportant, the ones she'd shoved so deep she'd eventually forgotten, slipped through her now. And fell together.

Her father had taken her to Whispering Oaks two days after their trip to Isle Dernier. He'd suggested a game of hide-and-seek....

Now Camille's fingers stung. Upstairs in the master chamber, the room where she and Jack had made love, she scraped her hands along the floorboards—and found the loose plank. It all stilled then, even as her heart pounded.

After over an hour of combing the old house, inspecting the floors and the walls, trying every stair on both staircases, she kneeled on the bare floor and closed her eyes, saw her dad.

Her throat burned. Her heart hurt. But she opened her eyes and pushed forward, worked at the board until it lifted—and saw the vault.

"Daddy," she whispered, because in that moment he was there, right beside her. Her hands wanted to shake, but she wouldn't let them, just reached inside and pulled out an old canvas knapsack—the one her father had brought with him to Isle Dernier.

And with the sun pouring in from the French doors, she reached inside—and felt the glass.

In 1789 darkness came to France. The Church became the enemy, the upper class the hunted, their possessions symbols of greed and inequity. Cathedrals and chapels were destroyed, nuns and priests executed. Chaos reigned.

In the northwestern province of Brittany, a noble family of deep faith saw the Reign of Terror destroying their beloved land and went to desperate measures to make sure their family survived. A son and a daughter were smuggled out of the country. With them, they carried a symbol of their family's legacy…a storied, beautifully crafted stained glass window from their family's chapel.

Now Camille rocked back on her heels and let the swell of warmth consume her. Her legacy. Her family. It had been her ancestors who had risked everything, her ancestors who'd made their way to Louisiana, who'd found a way to prosper. Her family who'd protected their legacy. Her family who'd been viewed with a mix of awe and suspicion…her family who the locals had turned to when they needed healing.

Her family who'd been forced to hide the stained glass during the darkest days of the Civil War.

Her grandmother's great-grandmother who'd taken the secret of the rapture with her to the grave.

Her father who'd died trying to reconstruct the clues…

"Oh, Daddy." The tears started. Hot and salty, they burned and flowed. "You found it…"

All this time, all these years, the stained glass window had been here all along.

Camille wasn't sure how long she sat on her knees tracing her finger along the exquisite depiction of angels and demons, sin and salvation. But she looked up when the creak of a floorboard broke the silence.

Saura. She stood and started for the door, stopped abruptly. *Because of the silence.* It rang through the still-ness—and sent her heart into a hard, unsteady rhythm.

There was no reason for her cousin to be quiet. No reason for her not to call out…

Maybe it was instinct. Or maybe just caution, her imagination. But on a sickening surge of adrenaline, Camille grabbed the stained glass and backed toward the French doors.

"You're talking about my mama, boy. No matter what y'think of me, ya can't really think I'd try to hurt her."

Jack kept his expression blank, his body still. But sitting across the small table from the man he'd once called father, the years fell away, and he could see Gator as he'd been a lifetime ago, walking up the steps to his mama's house with a bouquet of daisies in his hand. It had been Mother's Day. *Flowers,* he'd told his son. *Never forget to give your mama flowers.*

There'd been so many other moments, other kernels of advice. *Take care of your mama, boy. That's what a son does. Make her life easier, better.*

"If not you, then who?" Jack asked, but in his gut, he already knew. The fire had been set the night Marcel Lambert had put his plan against Gabe into motion. No one had connected the series of residential fires to Lambert, but all the pieces fell together now, and Jack realized his grandmother had almost lost everything as a result of a diversion.

"I wuz there that night," Gator said. "When I saw the smoke coming from the direction of Mama's house—"

They both turned as the door to the small interrogation room pushed open and his secretary hurried inside. "Sheriff, I know you didn't want to be disturbed, but—"

Jack stood, started toward her. Because of her voice, her eyes. The agitation. The nervousness. "What is it, MaryAnne?"

She lifted her arm, revealing the cordless phone in her hand. "Call came in a few minutes ago," she said. "I thought it was a crank at first, 'cuz no one was sayin' anything. But then—"

Jack didn't let her finish. He grabbed the handset and brought it to his face, went absolutely still.

"...don't force my hand, sweetheart."

And before another word was spoken, he started to run. Because Christ God Almighty, he knew. He knew that voice.

And he knew whose voice he would hear next.

Chapter 16

"Then don't force mine."

Her voice was strong and sure, with a steely resolve Jack recognized too well. "I'm not that scared little girl anymore, Marcel. I don't bend—and I don't break."

Jack grabbed his Glock and car keys, made for the door. "Get D'Ambrosia," he called to MaryAnne, then tossed the handset back to her. "Transfer it to my cell."

By the time he made it to his car, his phone was ringing—and Gator was sliding in beside him.

"I mean it, girl," Lambert said in that soft silky voice of his, without one trace of the Cajun accent he turned on so thick when the media hovered. "Not another step."

"Or what? You'll shoot?"

Dark spots clouded Jack's vision. He gunned the engine and flicked on the siren. Seven minutes. That's all he needed. If Camille could just keep him talking—

Camille. Christ. He'd let her walk away, had accused her of being reckless. But somehow she'd managed the 911 call.

She'd managed to call him.

"I don't think so," she said with not one flicker of fear in her voice. "Not this time."

"Put it down," Lambert instructed, and this time there was an edge to his voice. "Nice and slow."

Nice. And. Slow.

The words gunned through Jack. He accelerated onto the main highway, toward the drawbridge. He could use the siren for a few more minutes. Then: silence.

"Now why would I do that?" Camille asked, sugar-sweet, and goddamn it, everything inside Jack tightened. Through the blur of pine and cypress he could see them, standing somewhere at Whispering Oaks, each with a gun....

"Son—" Gator started, but Jack shot him a hard look.

"You really think I'm that stupid?" Camille asked— and Jack had never wanted to kiss her more. She was doing it, exactly what he needed her to do. Stalling, dragging out every minute. "You really think I'm naive enough to think you're going to let me walk away?"

"I did before."

"But not this time," Camille said. "Not now. The second I put this down, I'm a dead woman."

Jack flicked off the siren, but the speedometer continued to push one hundred. Dark thoughts raced faster. A gun didn't guarantee safety. Lambert could go for her thigh, her knee. One quick shot, and unless her reflexes—

"That's not true," Lambert said. "If I wanted to hurt you, I would have done that a long time ago. I've already told you. I'm just going to take you out into the woods. By the time they find you I'll be long gone."

Gone.

"You've killed before."

"It was an accident!" The edge to Lambert's voice finally broke. "Your sainted daddy lied to me. He told me he hadn't found the Rapture—"

"Because he knew you!" Camille shouted as Jack jerked the squad car into the opposite lane and veered past two pickups. "He knew you were going to take it, exploit it."

"He pulled the gun first, sweetheart."

"To protect himself—his family."

Jack turned hard onto the narrow dirt road to his right.

"You forget I was there," Camille went on. "I *heard!*"

"Stop here," Gator said, but Jack was already pulling off the road. They'd take the last half mile by foot.

"You were the one who charged him," Camille said. "You were the one who went after him."

Jack shoved open the door, and ran.

"You were the one who covered it up," she went on, more quietly this time. "You were the one who threatened Gator, ran him out of town, because he was there, too."

"Just put it down," Lambert said, and from the other man's voice, Jack knew he didn't have much longer.

"Because he saw, too," Camille said. "He knows."

Jack tore through the Spanish moss, ignored the tightness in his thigh.

"The man's a drunk," Lambert snarled.

"And you're a murderer," Camille said, still so goddamned calm.

"Go back," Jack called back to his father. "Wait for D'Ambrosia…don't let him drive in."

"So do it," Camille went on, and then Christ God have mercy, he saw her. Saw Camille. She stood with her back to the railing of the upper balcony with her arms outstretched, and in her hand—

Jack stopped. The breath, the truth, cut through him.

Through the heavily leafed branches of the oaks, sunlight glinted off the object in Camille's right hand.

"Shoot me," she invited and something inside of Jack started to unravel, "because so help me God you will never get your hands on this."

It all flashed then, and with blinding clarity Jack knew. She stood there, with her chin angled and her shoulders square, her hair whipping around her face—and the stained glass window held out like a sacrifice she was perfectly willing to make.

"Now who's the fool?"

Camille pressed her back to the old balustrade, knew what she had to do.

"You really think I believe you're just going to drop it?" Lambert asked, and this time the tall, once-elegant man moved. He took a step toward her. Then another. "You really expect me to believe you're going to let go, let it fall?" Something not quite right glittered in his eyes. "Let it break?"

Bluffing, she told herself. He was bluffing. "Absolutely."

A hard, distorted sound broke from his throat. "I don't think so."

The smooth edges of the glass her father had given his life to find burned against her flesh. "There's only one way to find out," she said. But God, her heart kicked hard. She had no way of knowing exactly how much time had passed since Lambert had tracked her onto the balcony. She'd fumbled in her purse, tried to get off the call.

But had no way of knowing if the call had gone through.

Or if MaryAnne would realize what was going on. The operator might not have heard anything, might have dismissed the call as a prank....

She couldn't stall much longer.

Eyes flat, Lambert used his free hand to unclip the phone at his waist, then jabbed a number. "Get in position," he instructed, then flipped the phone closed. All the while, he kept his eyes on Camille. "You're so like him," he snarled. "Proud to the end."

Her smile was slow, sure, but she said nothing, just watched him take another step.

"It didn't have to be like this," he said, as the wind whipped at them both.

"Oh, but it did." Too many nasty ends still dangled. Until they were tied off, she and Jack could never fully move forward. "My family," she said. "My rules." Slowly, she released her pinkie and middle finger, leaving the stained glass dangling between her thumb and forefinger. "And this time—"

From the room behind him, a shadow shifted...and Jack emerged.

The rush came hard and fast, but she banked it, hid it. "This time you won't be walking away," she promised as Jack moved toward them, slow, steady, like the soldier he'd been, the sheriff he was—the man he'd become. Shadows stole detail, but she didn't need to see, not when she felt the quickening deep in her blood.

Lambert's eyes narrowed. For a fleeting heartbeat he glanced beyond her, toward the ground below. Then he smiled—and without looking, Camille knew someone stood below.

Ready to catch the stained glass.

"You should have taken the out I gave you," Lambert taunted, but Camille didn't react, barely let herself breathe. Not when Jack stepped onto the balcony and inched toward them, slow and steady and so impossibly focused the pounding of her heart hurt. He gestured toward her, let her know he wanted her to duck.

"I don't take outs," she said as Jack held up three fingers. "And I don't run." Two fingers. "But you should have."

He laughed—

One finger.

—and lunged.

She twisted and pulled the stained glass to her side, dropped to her knees as Jack dived for Lambert. Swinging toward her, he jerked back violently—and momentum took over. In slow horrible motion she saw Lambert stagger...saw Jack reach for him. Saw the hundred-and-fifty-year-old railing crumble.

Saw Lambert vanish over the edge.

Heard the sickening thud.

And for a frozen moment she could do nothing, just kneel there clutching the stained glass window as the warm wind lashed at her and Jack. She looked up at him, saw the dark horror in his eyes, and felt what was left of her heart shatter.

But just as quickly the moment released them and he was reaching for her, even as she was pushing to her feet.

They met somewhere in the middle and reached for each other, and this time, they held on tight.

And so it came full circle. Years went by. The children grew into adults. But they never forgot, and they never gave up. They pushed forward and they healed...but not all the way. Not while loose ends dangled—and Marcel Lambert walked free.

Camille looked up from her keyboard and swiveled the big leather chair toward the large window behind the desk that dominated the Robichaud family study. The purplish hues of twilight stole detail, but not the crunch of tires against gravel.

Her heart rate quickened. Hours had passed since Saura had driven Camille to the family's secluded estate, where she was supposed to be resting. But too much energy surged through her. She couldn't curl up on a bed and go to sleep, not when...

Marcel Lambert was dead. After all these years, the man who'd taken her father's life had finally met his fate. He'd died a coward's death, breaking his neck when he went over the edge. No small irony there. She and Jack had run to the broken railing, had looked down to see Jack's father standing a few feet from Lambert's body...with a gun on Russ. Russ, the young deputy Jack had been grooming—Russ, the mole Lambert had planted in the sheriff's department to keep his ears and eyes open. Russ, who'd set the fire near Jack's grandmother's house...Russ, who'd stolen her laptop...who'd apprised Lambert of every step she'd taken.

Russ, who'd broken into her hotel room and read her notes, who'd notified Lambert she was on her way to Whispering Oaks.

The shock of it all...she'd felt it tear through Jack, felt him go so horribly still. She'd put a hand to his back and braced herself, knew fully well that he'd pull away. That he didn't want a hand to his back.

Instead he'd turned to her and lifted a hand to her face, slid the hair from her eyes. "It needs to end," he'd said in that awful, quiet voice. "Here, now...it needs to end."

And then D'Ambrosia had run onto the balcony, followed by Hank and several other deputies. And Saura. Saura had been there. She'd put her arms around Camille and held her, had never left her side, not at the plantation, not at the station, not even when Camille had given her statement. Jack—

Footsteps sounded against the marble entryway. Camille spun toward the door as it pushed open—and saw him.

Not Jack, but her heart sang anyway. And his name came on a quiet sob. "Gabriel."

Her brother strode toward her, and all that emotion she'd been keeping bottled up, the shock and the grief and the horror, broke free. She slipped from behind the desk and ran across the thick rug, launched herself into his arms.

"Camille," he whispered against the side of her face, but he didn't release her, not for a long, long time. He just held her tight, held her close. "God, Camille."

Her eyes filled. He'd been in college when she left for Florida. He'd been tall and gangly, with dreams in his eyes. Now he was a man, tall and so much like her father that her heart ached. At thirty-five, Gabe was almost the exact age their father had been....

She pulled back and looked up at him, didn't try to stop the tears from slipping over her lashes. "You're really here."

"Jack called last night."

Her heart broke a little more. "He's gone," she said. "Lambert is finally gone."

The brown of Gabe's eyes darkened. "But you did it," he said. "You got the confession."

"And the stained glass."

The voice came from the doorway—and it belonged to Jack. She looked beyond her brother to see him standing there, impossibly tall, so tired and brutally handsome that the breath jammed in her throat. An odd light glowed in his eyes. And in his hands he held the object her father had died to protect. "Jacques."

Gabe stepped back and slid his hand to hers, squeezed. "You did good, sis."

She tried to smile, but it hurt.

"Give us a few minutes?" Jack asked, but he didn't move, not until Gabe pressed a kiss to her cheek and turned to cross the study. Only after the sound of Gabe's footfalls faded did Jack step inside—and close the door. "Saura says you didn't sleep."

"Couldn't," she said. "Thought I'd get some of this down on paper while it was still—"

"Don't."

The force of that one word stopped her. He moved then, crossed toward her, his steps slow, controlled, deliberate, just as he did everything.

Until he reached her.

Until he reached the sofa by which she stood. Then that punishing veil of self-control fractured, and his eyes burned. He reached for her, put his hands to her shoulders and urged her toward him, but she was already moving, stepping into him as he tilted her face toward his.

His hands found the sides of her face as their mouths met, and any restraint that remained, any tiny crumb, fell away. The kiss was hard and deep and possessive, with no finesse or control, no discipline, only the raw need of a man who no longer wanted to pretend. A man who no longer wanted to deny.

A man who wanted to hold on.

On a dizzying rush Camille slid her arms around him and opened to him, wondered how she'd ever thought she could walk away from this man.

"Do you have any idea," he muttered against her mouth. "Any idea at all what it did to me to hear you on that phone…"

She slid a hand to his jaw, pressed her fingers to the soft prickle of whiskers. "We're here now…we're safe."

"To know that you were there with him," he went on, and then he pulled back and she could see his eyes, and in them she could see it all, feel it all. And she knew she'd never be able to close any doors, not when it came to this man. "And that I'd let you walk away—"

"Jack," she whispered, "you don't have to do this."

But something hard and broken flashed through his gaze. "I broke your heart," he rasped. "Fourteen years ago, when I walked away…"

She swallowed against the emotion crowding her throat. "You never made me any promises—"

"But then you walked away," he pressed on, and now

his eyes looked lit from the inside out. "And broke my heart even more."

That stopped her. That…floored her. She stepped back and looked up at him, felt what was left of her heart break into thousands of little pieces. "I don't understand…"

"Neither did I," he said. "Not until you came back. All these years—Christ. I've been frozen inside, holding on so damn tight, afraid to let go, afraid if I let so much as one variable spin away from me—"

She put a finger to his mouth—and smiled. "You never were too fond of dragons."

But slowly he shook his head. "That's where you're wrong, *'tite chat*. I craved those dragons. I craved—" He bit the words off as the lines of his face tightened. "They made me feel alive," he said. "*You* made me feel alive."

She realized it then, realized what he'd been fighting for so long. Not her, but himself. And his determination to never let obsession guide him, as it had guided his father. To never bow to it, to never bend. Break.

To never be weak.

"And then you were gone," he said, "and it was like going through the motions."

"Jack…"

"No one's ever come back before."

She stilled. "What?"

"No one's ever come back before—but then there you were," he pressed, and his hands were still on her face, his fingers spread wide. "At Whispering Oaks. And it all started to unravel."

She scraped her finger along the line of his jaw. "I thought I could come back," she said. "I thought I could come back and close all those doors…."

His fingers slid against her hair, and tangled. "That's why I pushed you away." He paused, lowered his voice. "That's why I lied to you about the map—to prove that I was still in control."

The truth whispered through her, and the dream, the one she'd smothered all those years ago, breathed again. "It wasn't the lie, Jack. That's not why I walked away— it was me." She could see it now, what she'd not let herself see before. "I latched onto the lie because it was easier, it was nice and tidy. But it was me…the fact that I'd done it again, that I hadn't closed a single door…that I was still just as vulnerable to you as I'd always been."

That's why she'd walked away.

"But I was wrong," she said. "I know that now. I don't want to close doors, Jack. I want to walk through them—with you."

His smile was slow, languorous, so pure classic Jacques Savoie that her heart ached. He stepped back from her and took her hand, urged her toward the door leading from the study. And opened it. "Then what do you say we get started?"

Epilogue

"**D**ad said it was like stepping into a Monet painting."

Jack looked from the rugged field of ancient monoliths to the quaint chapel tucked at the bottom of the French hillside. "Guess we know where your flare for drama came from."

Grinning, Camille took a long sip from her water bottle before returning it to her backpack. The planning was over. Tonight they would move forward.

"He liked the colors," she said, glancing to the west, where the remains of the sun put on a show. Located in far Northwest France, Brittany was an odd mix of coastline and ancient towns and inland woods. "Said it was like walking through a picture book."

Jack picked up his binoculars and studied the chapel. The last visitor had left thirty minutes before. "You ready?" he asked.

Kneeling there in the vivid green grass, she slid a hand to the knapsack beside her. "Not yet."

For almost a week they'd been observing the chapel, monitoring who came and who went, whether any security was in place. And like clockwork, a grounds-keeper locked up with the sunset and the old church sat quiet until morning came.

The first day they'd gone inside—and seen the window. It was just one of many, a complete reproduction of the stained glass windows that had once adorned the chapel, back before the days of the French Revolution, when any symbol of Christianity had been methodically destroyed.

The chapel, in Camille's family for hundreds of years, had survived. Only the windows had been destroyed.

They'd stood there while several older women had kneeled at the altar and prayed, and a young boy had played pick-up-sticks. They'd compared the image mounted six feet off the ground with the pictures they'd taken of the original—and they knew no one would ever suspect.

Only a handful knew. Camille and Jack, Saura and D'Ambrosia, Gabe and his fiancée, Evangeline. Jack's father. They knew. Marcel did, too, but he was dead. And Russ...Russ had no idea of the significance or the legend...no idea the stained glass was what Lambert had coveted all along.

What Camille's father had wanted—what Jack's father had wanted.

Returning it to Brittany had been Camille's idea, and it felt right. Too many lives had been destroyed. Too much blood shed. There was no point making their discovery public.

"Look, there it is," she said, and he turned toward the east, where a near-full moon hovered low on the horizon.

But it wasn't the moon that had Jack sliding his hand into his pocket, his fingers curling around the small velvet box. They'd spent two days in Paris. And while Camille had strolled through a small boutique, Jack had made a detour.

Now he watched her, and all those loose ends quietly fell together. Twenty years had passed since he'd last seen that glow in her eyes. The warmth and contentment and—peace. She'd been a girl then. She'd worn pigtails and cutoffs and had foolishly hung curtains in his tree-fort. And he'd spent his time playing baseball and listening to records, helping out his grandmother and loving…Camille. Like a sister, he'd always told himself.

Like a sister.

She was a woman now, with sleek blond hair and hip-hugging jeans, a career as a bestselling true crime writer. She'd finished her book. It would come out with the new year.

And he was sheriff. He had a town to take care of. And a home. A family—and a father. It would take time, but when Jack looked in the mirror and saw the dark brown of his eyes, he no longer looked away.

They could never go back to before, not any of them.

But they could go forward.

"Come here," he said hoarsely.

She glanced back at him and damn near slayed him with the glow in her eyes. "Why?"

"Maybe I have a surprise."

The wind blew hair against her face. "We've got all night," she said. "What's the hurry?"

Against the box, his fingers tightened. "Come on over and I'll show you."

Her smile was slow, easy. "That sounds an awful lot like an invitation," she said, stretching just so, settling down with her head propped on her hand—and the curve of her body sprawled against the grass.

She was right. They had all night. The summer solstice was the shortest of the year, that was true. But there was still plenty of time—and not a soul in sight. "Tryin' to torture me, *'tite chat?*"

"Torture?" she asked, sliding her pinkie along her lower lip. "What happened to Mr. Nice-and-Slow-Is-Best?"

He put the binoculars down. And stood. "You," he said. "You happened." Then he went to her.

And showed her what she'd showed him—just how good a little chaos could be.

* * * * *

*Mills & Boon® Intrigue brings you a sneak
preview of Caridad Piñeiro's
Secret Agent Reunion…*

*A mysterious betrayal led super spy Danielle
Moore to fake her own death. Now she is ready
to re-emerge and seek vengeance. But things
get complicated when she realises a mole in her
agency is still leaking vital information – and her
new partner is an ex-lover she thought was dead.*

*Don't miss the fantastic second story
in the thrilling*
MISSION: IMPASSIONED
*series, available next month in
Mills & Boon® Intrigue!*

Secret Agent Reunion
by
Caridad Piñeiro

Only someone who had come back from the dead truly knew how deadly distractions could be.

Danielle Moore had let personal feelings get in the way of a top-secret mission over a year ago and had nearly lost her life. So she kept her eyes glued to the man—six feet two inches of thick muscle—as he charged at her like a linebacker after a quarterback, arms outstretched to trap her in his embrace.

Dani used his momentum against him, sweeping him aside with a matador like step. Turning quickly as he stumbled by, she snapped an elbow to the back of his neck and dropped him to the ground. Before she could totally incapacitate him, another more compact man charged at her from the opposite side of the room.

She pushed off the first man's fallen body and came up ready for action, but as she did so, something pulled along her midsection. A twinge of pain followed, but she tamped it down. She couldn't allow physical discomfort or weakness to divert her attention.

As the smaller man shoved past his rising friend, she released a sharp dropkick, catching him squarely in the chest and rocking him backward, where he immediately tripped over the larger man. Both men sprawled to the ground in a messy heap.

Dani stopped, placed her hands on her hips and laughed as they tried to untangle themselves and resume their attack.

"Come on, boys. Is that the best you can do?" she teased in fluent French.

After months of training together, the three of them had developed an easy camaraderie. Even now, when the men couldn't seem to contain Dani as her physical strength and martial arts prowess returned rapidly, they accepted her superior abilities good-naturedly.

Her current physical state was quite different from what it had been nearly three months ago, Dani thought.

After being shot and lingering in a coma off and on, she had emerged long enough to approve the removal of the bullet that had lodged precariously close to her spine. Three months after that, she had finally been well enough to begin physical therapy and try to get back into shape.

She had a new mission waiting for her, after all. At least, that's what the enigmatic man by her bedside had intimated to her so many months ago.

Dani now knew who that mysterious angel was—Corbett Lazlo, the elusive powerhouse behind the Lazlo Group, a private agency known for handling the most discreet and sometimes dangerous of missions. A group well known to her from her time with the Secret Intelligence Service, or SIS, the British equivalent of the CIA and the agency at which she had worked as the Sparrow, a world-renowned assassin.

Only she hadn't really been an assassin. All her supposed "kills" had been taken into SIS custody so that SIS might find out more information about an elusive crime organization they called SNAKE, which they suspected of being responsible for a number of illegal operations.

She had let her last mission get personal. Her actions had resulted in the death of the prince of Silvershire and had nearly caused her death and that of her twin sister. SIS had been less than pleased that, in her quest to find her parents' killers, she had messed up the mission in Silvershire, the small European island kingdom she had called home at one time. With her cover as the Sparrow possibly blown and an international incident brewing, SIS had tossed her out.

Lazlo, who had also been thrown out of SIS many years earlier, was the man she had to thank for keeping her alive. He was the one responsible for the medical treatment that had worked a miracle and brought her back from the dead.

He had taken her into his agency and told her that he would let her know when the time was right for her to be reborn and go out on another mission.

She felt mission-ready now and sensed that somehow Lazlo would know that.

He seemed to know everything about everyone while she, like most of the people she had met within his group, knew little about him. To her surprise, few had even seen the elusive Mr. Lazlo.

After thanking her two sparring partners for the training session, she walked to the gym to finish her workout. She took a place at the first station and lifted the weights, evenly pushing up the bars on the bench press and enjoying the strength she had regained in her arms. Satisfied, she finished her reps and moved on to the next station and then the next.

By the time she finished, her muscles trembled from her exertions, but it was a good feeling. The kind of sore that said she was getting stronger.

The kind of pain that confirmed she was still alive.

In the locker room, she peeled off her clothes and grabbed a towel, ready for a long soak in the Jacuzzi. As she passed a mirror, she stopped short, surprised by what stared back at her.

The image of a hard-bodied woman of average height was reflected in the mirror. Shoulder-length hair in need of a trim. Fine-boned shoulders leading to full breasts above a long, barely pink scar that ran down her middle. Beside the scar was the ragged, stellar-shaped wound where she had been shot during her last mission.

The physical wounds of the past year were alive in her vision, much like those in her heart, which had been there far longer. The scar of her parents' murder. The ragged and still unhealed wound from her lover's death barely three years ago.

Dani ran her hand down the long scar, but it was numb. Just as she was numb inside. Paralyzed. Yet she still had things to do so that might make her feel alive again.

So that she could finally go home. Go and see her twin sister, Elizabeth.

Only, as she'd heard before, she suspected that she could never truly go home again.

Lazlo agent Mitch Lama watched as Dani sparred with the two men in the gym.

Was she ready? he wondered tapping his lips with his index finger as Dani deftly handled the two much larger men.

The frailness from her injuries was gone, as was the pallor that had colored her skin for the many months she had been unconscious and battling for life. Months during which he had come to sit by her bedside, urging her to keep up the fight. Reading to her in hopes that she might hear his voice and return because they had things to settle between them.

Now she was back from the dead and he didn't know what to do with her. What to do about the lies she had told him for so long. Lies that had nearly cost him his life and hers.

She looked strong now. Presumably ready for action.

He had always admired Dani's physicality. Been intrigued by the strength beneath the seemingly fragile and feminine surface.

She was a warrior. A champion who was forever prepared to take up a cause and fight a wrong.

He both loved and hated her for being a hero.

For nearly three years, he had been waiting to see her. To talk to her again. To be able to touch her and have her know it was him.

To ask her why she had lied to him about who she was, even as he'd lain dying.

A loud beep came from his computer, notifying him that he had an urgent message from Corbett Lazlo. A second later, his phone rang and he had no doubt who would be on the line.

He shut down his access to the camera trained on Dani, immediately regretting the loss of her.

"Lama," he said, a tinge of annoyance in his voice that he had been pulled away from his surveillance.

Corbett Lazlo identified himself. "Did you get my message?"

"Hold on just one second, sir, while I open it," he said, the cadence and tone from his days in the military coloring his speech. He double-clicked to open the e-mail message Lazlo had forwarded and held his breath as he read it.

The message threatened with its simplicity.

Ready for Round 2?

"I'm assuming Cordez couldn't track the source of this message either?" He wondered why their top computer person was having such difficulty tracing the mysterious missives.

"You're correct. Plus, I have some other news."

He knew the news would be bad so he preempted Lazlo's report. "Another operative is down. I'm assuming the same MO as before?"

"Unfortunately, yes. His body was discovered not far from our Prague offices. Close-range shot to the head, just above the left ear. Hollow-point bullet. I've asked our various contacts to see if they have a record of any assassins with a similar MO but I suspect there may be quite a few."

Mitch considered the facts and sensed that the moment for waiting and watching had ended. Time for him and the Sparrow to join forces and discover who was behind the messages and attacks.

"I'm assuming that you want me to activate the Lazarus Liaison now, Mr. Lazlo."

Silence came across the line before Lazlo asked, "Do you think she's ready?"

He recalled the sight of Dani as she sparred. "I think she's physically ready, sir."

"Quite the political answer. And you? Are you ready? Physically? Emotionally?"

He'd be a liar if he said "yes," and so he provided the only answer he could.

"That remains to be seen, sir."

FREE

4 BOOKS AND A SURPRISE GIFT!

We would like to take this opportunity to thank you for reading this Mills & Boon® book by offering you the chance to take FOUR more specially selected titles from the Intrigue series absolutely FREE! We're also making this offer to introduce you to the benefits of the Mills & Boon® Book Club™—

- ★ **FREE home delivery**
- ★ **FREE gifts and competitions**
- ★ **FREE monthly Newsletter**
- ★ **Books available before they're in the shops**
- ★ **Exclusive Mills & Boon Book Club offers**

Accepting these FREE books and gift places you under no obligation to buy; you may cancel at any time, even after receiving your free shipment. Simply complete your details below and return the entire page to the address below. You don't even need a stamp!

YES! Please send me 4 free Intrigue books and a surprise gift. I understand that unless you hear from me, I will receive 6 superb new titles every month for just £3.15 each, postage and packing free. I am under no obligation to purchase any books and may cancel my subscription at any time. The free books and gift will be mine to keep in any case.

I8ZEE

Ms/Mrs/Miss/Mr..Initials ....

BLOCK CAPITALS PLEASE

Surname ....

Address ....

....

....Postcode ....

Send this whole page to:
The Mills & Boon Book Club, FREEPOST CN81, Croydon, CR9 3WZ